# SHANNON'S RIDE

# A
# Clay Shannon
# Western

# SHANNON'S RIDE

•

## Charles E. Friend

***AVALON BOOKS***
NEW YORK

PRINTED IN THE UNITED STATES OF AMERICA
ON ACID-FREE PAPER
BY HADDON CRAFTSMEN, BLOOMSBURG, PENNSYLVANIA

This book is dedicated to the men and women,
military and civilian, who at the time of this writing
are daily placing themselves "in harm's way" defending our
country from its enemies.

## Chapter One

Clay Shannon stood by the ornate iron railing of the second-floor balcony, savoring the aroma of the morning's first cup of coffee as he watched the dawn breaking over Rancho Alvarez. Like most New Mexico sunrises, this one was spectacular, and Shannon watched with pleasure as the brilliant red and gold light came creeping across the eastern sky toward the hacienda.

"Lovely, isn't it?" a soft voice said from the bedroom doorway behind him. Charlotte Alvarez Shannon walked onto the balcony, still in her nightdress, and stood beside Shannon holding his arm tightly as the sun slowly cleared the horizon and started its climb toward the new day.

Shannon looked down at his wife and smiled. In any light Charlotte was a beautiful woman, but in the golden

1

glow of the morning she was, he decided, even more beautiful than the sunrise itself.

"There's something magical about this time of the morning," Charlotte murmured. "It's so fresh and clean, and so very peaceful."

"Let's hope it stays peaceful," Shannon said wryly. "We've had enough unpeaceful days around here to last a lifetime."

Charlotte nodded, remembering. Scarcely a year ago, the walled garden below them had echoed with the sound of gunfire, and the scent of the flowering bushes had for a time been overpowered by the acrid smell of gunsmoke as she and Shannon and the vaqueros of Rancho Alvarez fought desperately to beat back the attackers who had been sent by a madman to kill them.

"That seems so long ago now," she said quietly. "In another time, almost in another world. Perhaps because we suffered so much then, we've earned the right to enjoy peace and happiness now."

"Perhaps," said Shannon slowly. "Perhaps not."

Charlotte sensed a sudden alertness in his manner, and saw that he was now leaning on the railing, staring intently at the horizon.

"What is it?" she asked.

"Rider coming," he replied in a flat voice.

Charlotte shaded her eyes, following his gaze. A horseman had appeared over a distant rise, dust swirling behind him as he galloped headlong toward the hacienda. Even at that distance they could see that the man was bent forward in the saddle, driving the horse toward them with an unmistakable urgency.

Shannon turned and went back into the bedroom, buttoning his shirt. His gunbelt was hanging from its hook near the door, and he swung it around his waist, buckling it with an easy motion born of many years of practice. Quickly he drew the ivory-handled Colt out of the holster, checked the cylinder, then slid the six-gun back into the leather, hefting the weapon slightly to be sure that it was free for immediate use if needed. Charlotte, now dressing rapidly, saw the familiar motion and felt a sudden chill touching her heart, as if a cloud had passed over the sun.

Shannon was in the hallway now, headed for the broad staircase that led to the ground floor.

"Wait for me," Charlotte called. But Shannon did not wait.

She joined him on the verandah of the house just as the rider came galloping through the iron gates.

"It's Pablo," she said, recognizing one of their vaqueros.

"Yes," Shannon said in the same flat tone.

The rider pulled the tired horse to a halt in front of them and dismounted, removing his sombrero as he approached.

"What's wrong, Pablo?" Charlotte asked.

"Señora, Señor," Pablo said, trying to catch his breath. "I was on my way out to mend fences when I saw vultures in the sky to the west. Many vultures, Señor—more than I have ever seen before. They were circling over the valley of the Rio Verde. I turned back to tell you because I thought you should know."

Charlotte caught her breath. "That's where one of the herds is, Clay," she said. "Manuel moved them over there two days ago."

"I know," Shannon said grimly. "Pablo, please saddle my horse—the buckskin—and bring him up here to the house. We'll ride over there and take a look."

"I'm going too," Charlotte said. "I'll get our horses myself."

They rode toward the river at a fast canter with Shannon and Charlotte in the lead and Pablo trailing unhappily in the rear.

"Look," Charlotte said, pointing.

"I see them," Shannon said. Ahead, a dozen vultures were circling lazily above the hills, black against the sky.

They urged their horses forward and soon topped a rise that looked down into a large valley. Below them was the Rio Verde, the little tributary of the Pecos River whose muddy stream provided the herds of Rancho Alvarez with water. Normally it was a pretty place, with cattle peacefully grazing under the brilliant New Mexico sun and green trees lining the river.

Today, however, the scene was far from peaceful. Along the bank of the river lay the bodies of four men and a half-dozen cattle. There was blood on the ground, and a vulture was tearing at one of the steer carcasses.

"Oh, no," Charlotte cried, staring. "Oh, Clay . . ."

Shannon cursed and sent the buckskin stallion lunging down the hill, with Charlotte and Pablo close behind.

As he reached the bank of the river, Shannon swung out of the saddle and knelt down beside one of the fallen men.

"Who is it?" Charlotte said, dismounting beside him.

"It's Manuel," Shannon said. "He's been shot."

"Is he dead?" Charlotte asked in a broken voice. Manuel was the second vaquero of Rancho Alvarez, one of the oldest of the Alvarez family's retainers.

"I don't know yet," Shannon said, bending over the still form.

Pablo had dismounted behind them and was watching, wide-eyed.

"Pablo, check the others, will you?" Shannon said.

"*Sí,* Señor," Pablo said, crossing himself.

Shannon placed his arm under Manuel's shoulders and lifted him up a little, feeling for a heartbeat. It was there, faint but unmistakable.

"He's alive," Shannon said. "Manuel, can you hear me?"

Manuel moaned, then coughed and opened his eyes.

"Ah, *Patrón,*" he gasped. "It is you. *Gracias a Dios!*"

"What happened, Manuel?" Shannon asked quietly.

"A dozen men, perhaps more," Manuel said. "Yes, more I think. They came out of the darkness as we sat beside the campfire. We had no chance, Señor Shannon. None. They shot down Miguel and Fernando and Alejandro even as we tried to reach our rifles."

Shannon's face darkened with anger.

"Did you recognize any of them?" he said.

"No, Señor. *Lo siento mucho.* I am very sorry. It all happened so fast. Miguel went down immediately, then the others. I got to my rifle and fired back. I'm sure I wounded at least one of them. Then I was hit and fell too. Soon, I heard more gunshots—I think the *banditos* were stampeding the cattle. Finally, one of them came walking past, shooting all of us again as we lay on the ground. After that, I can remember nothing more. Forgive me—I have failed you and the señora. But I did get one of them, Señor Shannon. I did at least get one of them."

Shannon eased him back down to the ground.

"All right, Manuel," he said. "You did well. Rest now. We'll move you to the house as quickly as we can and attend to your wounds."

Pablo had been hesitantly checking the other bodies.

"They are all dead, Señor," he said in a broken voice. One of the dead men, Fernando, had been his cousin.

Shannon climbed to the top of the next rise and surveyed the surrounding area, then walked back down to the river where Charlotte was still trying to comfort Manuel.

"The cattle are gone," Shannon told her. "Not an animal in sight. Whoever those men were, they've gotten away with the whole south herd—two thousand head at least."

They all looked up as the sound of hoofbeats approached over the rise. Ramón Peralta, the ranch's chief vaquero, rode down the slope and dismounted, staring around him in disbelief at the carnage.

"I came as soon as I heard," he said. "*Madre de Dios,* what has happened here?"

Shannon told him.

They sent Pablo hurrying back to the hacienda to get a wagon in which to transport Manuel and the three dead men. Then, while Charlotte remained with Manuel, Shannon and Ramón rode slowly over the ground, studying the tracks of the vanished cattle.

"Headed southeast," Shannon said. "Hard to say how many riders, but I'd guess at least fifteen men. What do you think?"

"I agree," Ramón said. "At least fifteen, maybe more. They must have stampeded the cattle just as Manuel said, and then ridden after them. No doubt they rounded up as many as they could find in the darkness and then herded them away."

He leaned out of the saddle to inspect something on the ground.

"Look, Señor Shannon," he said. "Blood."

Shannon dismounted and examined the spots that lay among the hoofprints along the dry earth. The blood trail followed the tracks off to the southeast.

"Looks like Manuel really did wing one of them," Shannon said, climbing back into the saddle. "The tracks haven't covered the bloodstains, so the wounded man must have been following along behind the herd."

Ramón nodded in agreement.

"*Si,*" he said. "And there are many stains. He must be badly hurt."

"I certainly hope so," Shannon said bitterly. He glanced up at the sun. It was now midmorning.

"They already have at least twelve hours' start on us," he said. "Let's get going."

## Chapter Two

They carried Manuel and the bodies of the dead back to the ranch house in the wagon that Pablo had brought. The ground was rough, and the bouncing of the wagon caused the wounded vaquero great pain, but Manuel kept urging Pablo to go faster.

"We must hurry, Señor," he called to Shannon, who was riding beside the wagon. "We must go after the *banditos* at once if we are to catch up to them by nightfall."

"You won't be chasing any bandits for awhile, my friend," Shannon said. "But don't worry—we'll get them. If not by tonight, then by tomorrow night or the night after that or the night after that. However long it takes, rest assured, *amigo*—we'll get them."

Ramón had ridden on ahead to the hacienda. By the time the wagon reached the ranch house, all of the servants were gathered anxiously on the verandah, waiting. Miguel and Alejandro had been married; their wives began to weep piteously as they saw their husbands' bodies lying in the back of the wagon.

As carefully as possible, Shannon and several of the others lifted Manuel from the wagon bed and carried him inside. Ramón came from the back of the house carrying his rifle.

"All the vaqueros who are here are saddling their horses," Ramón said to Shannon. "I have sent riders out to find the rest of the men. Some of our people are away rounding up strays and working on the fence line, and of course many are out on the north and west ranges with the rest of the cattle. It may be many hours before we can call all of them in."

"We can't wait for them," Shannon said. "We'll start out with what we have, and the rest can follow."

He paused, remembering the dangers of the past.

"Be sure to leave enough men here to guard the hacienda and the remaining cattle," he added. "There may be other bandits nearby."

He rubbed his eyes, trying to gather his thoughts.

"Make certain that each of our men has weapons, ammunition, and food for several days," he said. "When they're mounted up, assemble them here in front of the house. I'll be ready in a few minutes."

As Ramón hurried away to make the preparations, Shannon reentered the house and climbed the stairs to the second floor. He went into the bedroom and removed a set of worn saddlebags from a closet. Moving quickly, he filled them with spare clothing and other necessities, then tossed a second revolver and two boxes of ammunition in on top before buckling down the flaps. Next, he went back to the heavy chest that stood against one wall of the room. Opening the top drawer, he reached in and removed a shining metal badge from its resting place. The words "U.S. Marshal" on the burnished metal were bright and clear in the sunlight that flooded into the room from the balcony outside.

Charlotte came into the room. Shannon held up the badge.

"I thought I was through wearing this," he said. "Now it seems that my life as a rancher has made it necessary for me to become a lawman again."

Charlotte smiled sadly.

"You never stopped being a lawman, Clay," she said. "You never will. It's been grand having you here these past months, but all along I've known that sooner or later that badge would come out of the drawer, and you would be Marshal Shannon again."

"The difference is, this time it's not just duty," Shannon replied. "This is personal. We have a herd to recover and a score to settle with the men who stole it. When that's done, the badge will go back into the drawer again."

He picked up the saddlebags.

"Now I have to go," he said. "The men will be waiting, and we've a lot of ground to cover."

"I'm coming with you," Charlotte said. "I'll get my things."

"No," Shannon said firmly. "Not this time, Charlotte. It's too dangerous."

Charlotte's dark eyes flashed.

"They're my cattle too," she said feelingly. "And those who died were my friends as well as yours. Besides, we've shared many dangers, you and I, and we've fought together before to protect what is ours."

Shannon took her in his arms and gently lifted her chin so that he could look directly into her face.

"I know," Shannon said. "But we have only a few men, and the outlaws have many. When we fight them, we may lose. If the rest of us went down, you would be left to the mercy of those killers, and I won't risk that. Stay here, Charlotte. Guard our people and our house and our land until I return. Please. It is my earnest wish."

Tears sprang into Charlotte's eyes. She nodded reluctantly.

"Very well," she said. "I'll stay—for now. But if you're gone too long, I will surely follow you, regardless of whatever danger there may be."

Shannon laughed.

"I know you will," he said. "You always do. But we won't be gone long, I hope. And the sooner I get going, the sooner I can come home again."

He pinned the U.S. marshal's badge securely to his coat, picked up the saddlebags, and went quickly down the stairs. As he did so, he felt a twinge of guilt. He did not want to leave Charlotte, but while he was pinning on the badge he experienced once again the old excitement, the familiar thrill of the chase that had made him a lawman for twenty years. In a strange sort of way, he was glad to be wearing the badge again.

*Besides,* he thought, *it's as I told Charlotte—this is more than just another job. This is personal—very personal.*

## Chapter Three

They rode back to the river to pick up the trail of the stolen cattle. Turning southeast to follow the tracks, they pushed their horses steadily along, trying to make up ground. There were only nine of them altogether. Ramón rode beside Shannon, leading the seven ranch hands that were all that had been available on short notice. Messages had been sent out across the range to the other men of Rancho Alvarez to follow as soon as they could. In a few hours, a day at most, a dozen more vaqueros would be riding after them, well armed and ready to fight. Until then, Shannon would have to be careful, for it was apparent that if they caught up to the rustlers too soon, they would be far outnumbered. Shannon badly wanted to overtake the outlaws, but he had no intention of getting his little band massacred. Caution would be required until the rest of his men arrived.

The country through which they were riding became progressively more dry and desolate, for Rancho Alvarez was located at the southern edge of New Mexico's best grazing country. Beyond, toward the Mexican border, lay a more desolate region and, ultimately, the great Sonora Desert. Fortunately, despite the growing harshness of the land, the many hundreds of cattle that made up the south herd had left tracks a blind man could follow, even over the rocky ground.

Despite the obviousness of the trail, or perhaps because of it, Shannon was uneasy. The broken country through which they were passing could easily hide a hostile presence from their view. As a precaution, he sent two of the vaqueros out to watch their flanks while he and Ramón rode well in advance of the other men, setting the pace and watching the trail ahead.

They rode in grim silence, each man thinking of what lay behind, and what might lie ahead. An hour passed, then two. Occasionally they saw steers wandering through the sparse vegetation, unbranded strays that had not yet been collected into the Alvarez herd. Then, at last, the black line of a barbed wire fence became visible ahead, marking the ultimate boundary of Rancho Alvarez. The cattle tracks led up to and through the fence line. Several sections of the wire had been cut and the fence posts pulled down, creating a broad gap through which the cattle had passed.

"Leave a man behind to repair the wire," Shannon said as they rode through the break. "He can follow us when he's done."

Ramón detailed one of the vaqueros to the task. The man protested at being left behind, but Shannon remained firm. He did not want to lose any more cattle through a broken fence.

On they went, but despite their steady pace there was no sign that they were overtaking their quarry.

"Wherever they're headed, they must have gotten a good start on us," Shannon observed to Ramón. "They can't move that many cattle very fast, and we've made good time."

"They must know that we will follow them," Ramón mused. "They may take precautions."

"Oh, yes," Shannon said. "Odds are they'll leave men behind to ambush us somewhere along the way. It's what I'd do if I were in their boots."

"Soon they will die in their boots," Ramón said darkly, touching the knife that he wore in his belt.

Shannon shivered involuntarily. He had seen what Ramón could do with a knife.

Another hour passed. Shannon shifted uncomfortably in his saddle, trying to ease the ache that was starting to creep through his body.

*I've been a* patrón *too long,* he thought. *Living a soft life while other men did the riding. Just as well that I'm doing some of the work myself again.*

Abruptly, one of the flankers turned his horse and came riding back to the trail.

"What is it, Carlos?" Shannon asked as the man pulled up beside him.

"*Muchos buitres,* Señor," Carlos replied. "In the sky to the southeast. You can see them from that hill."

*More buzzards,* Shannon thought. *Who or what has died now?*

The cattle trail led up a small hill, and soon Shannon saw what Carlos had seen—the black silhouettes of the birds of prey as they wheeled lazily above something that lay beyond the next rise.

"Spread out," Shannon said to the vaqueros, "and go slowly. There may be trouble ahead."

Rifles drawn, the party moved cautiously up the rise and paused at the top. In the depression below them a saddled horse, reins dragging, was foraging listlessly in the sparse vegetation. On the ground near the animal, a human form was stretched out upon the hard earth, unmoving.

Shannon's eyes swept the ridges around them, searching for signs of danger, but there was no evidence of any hostile presence in the rocks. He sent several of the vaqueros out along the ridge line as a precaution, then rode down with Ramón to the spot where the man's body lay on its back in the dust.

"He is dead, I think," Ramón said.

"So it seems," replied Shannon. Even from a distance he could see that the man was staring sightlessly at the afternoon sky. Nearby, a vulture was perched expectantly on the limb of a small tree, watching them with its cold, beady eyes.

As they approached, the vulture reluctantly took wing, flapping away to a safe distance and coming to rest upon a boulder from which it could safely view the unwelcome intruders who had interrupted its anticipated dinner.

Shannon stepped down out of the saddle and leaned over the corpse.

"I know this man," he said.

Ramón dismounted and stood beside him.

"Who is he?" he asked, scowling at the cadaver.

"His name is Finch. He was one of the gunmen we ran out of Los Santos last year."

Ramón's eyes narrowed in recognition.

"I remember him now," he said. "He worked for Señor Kruger, the man who tried to take over the town. You and the townspeople put Kruger's gunmen on their horses and told them to leave New Mexico, never to return."

"Apparently he didn't heed our advice," Shannon remarked absently, staring at the hole low down in the man's bloody shirt. "He must be the one Manuel shot last night," he added. "Well, he won't be coming to Los Santos again."

He began going through the dead man's pockets. The search produced nothing but a plug of chewing tobacco, a pocketknife, and a bent silver dollar.

"Strange that his friends didn't stay behind to help him," said Ramón warily, eyeing the cliffs above where the Rancho Alvarez vaqueros were now standing guard. "They didn't even take his horse with them."

"He probably lagged behind," Shannon said. "Chances are that by the time he fell off the horse and died, the others were already miles away."

He prodded the body with the toe of his boot. "Been dead several hours, I'd say," he said, noting the stiffness of the dead man's limbs. "His friends must still have a good lead on us. Well, leave a couple of men to bury him—they can catch up with us when they're finished. We need to keep moving."

"What about the man's horse, *Patrón?*"

"Unsaddle it and turn it loose—it should be all right. It won't wander far, and the rest of our people can pick it up when they come along."

Ramón was studying the cattle tracks again.

"They keep moving to the southeast," he said. "Soon they will reach the Rio Pecos. Perhaps they intend to take the cattle into Texas."

"Possibly," Shannon said. "They may plan to sell them somewhere close to the Texas border, or they might drive them on further east to the cattle buyers at the railroad. They could even turn south and head for Mexico."

"If they go into Mexico, will we follow them?" Ramón asked, looking dubiously at the badge on Shannon's coat. As a U.S. marshal, Shannon would have no law enforcement powers in Mexico.

"Oh, yes," Shannon replied. "We'll follow them wherever they go. If they cross the Rio Grande, we'll go into Mexico after them. As far as it takes, and as long as it takes."

He unbuckled the dead man's gunbelt and passed it to Ramón.

"Some of our men don't have revolvers," he said. "Give this to one of them—whoever is the best shot. And bring the rifle off that horse's saddle. Before we're through with this trip, we may need all the guns we can get."

## Chapter Four

They rode all day and through most of the night, stopping only once for a brief interval to rest the horses. The journey was long and dusty, and by the afternoon of the second day both men and mounts were tiring noticeably. They had ridden hard, and Shannon knew that they could not go on indefinitely.

"How far to the Pecos now, Ramón?" he asked.

Ramón squinted up at the sun, now starting its descent toward the western horizon.

"Two hours, I think. Perhaps three. We have covered many miles—more than I would have thought possible in so short a time."

Shannon reached for his canteen and shook it. It was nearly empty.

"Are there any water holes between us and the Pecos?" he said.

"No, *Patrón,*" Ramón replied. "None that I know of."

"Then we'd better hope we find the river soon. These horses need water and so do we."

They reached the Pecos River at twilight. This far into New Mexico the Pecos was not as wide as it was further to the south where it crossed into Texas, but in that dry country it was still a substantial body of water. Shannon halted the men well short of the river, then rode alone down to the riverbank. Even in the failing light he could see the hoofprints of the stolen herd in the mud at the water's edge. Shannon rode back up the hill to the crest where the others were waiting.

"They've beaten us to it," he said. "But not by much, from the look of the tracks."

"We will cross now?" Ramón asked hopefully.

Shannon stared out across the shallow stream toward the boulders on the other side. They were already in deep shadow, and in the gathering darkness it was impossible to tell if anyone was lying in wait among them.

"No," Shannon said. "If I were a bunch of killers on the run, this is where I'd leave some men behind to discourage any pursuit. There could be a dozen riflemen in those rocks, just waiting to catch us out in the middle of the river, exposed to their fire. We'll wait until morning. I don't like it, but it's the smart play. At least in daylight we'll be able to see who's shooting at us. And by then the rest of our men should have joined us. When we finally lock horns with the rustlers, I want to make certain that we have enough firepower to do the job properly."

The vaqueros grumbled a little when Remón informed them that they would camp for the night on the west side of the river. However, their fierce desire to catch up to the men who had murdered their friends and stolen their *patrón's* cattle was tempered by the weariness of two days and a night spent almost continuously in the saddle. And, in any event, they recognized that Shannon was right—it would be better to cross in daylight, after they had been reinforced by the remainder of the Rancho Alvarez vaqueros.

As the twilight deepened, they made their camp at the top of the hill beside the river. They dared not light a fire, so their evening meal would be beef jerky and cold beans and their bed a thin blanket on stony ground, but these were hard men well accustomed to cold food and spartan conditions, and no one complained.

Ramón had been prowling around by the riverbank, studying the tracks in the last of the failing light. At length he rode back up the hill, tied his horse, and sat down beside Shannon where the latter was just finishing his unappetizing dinner.

"Señor Shannon," said the foreman, "there are the hoof-marks of several riders moving away toward the southeast on this bank of the river. I followed them as far as I could before it became too dark to see. There were at least three horses, perhaps four—I could not be certain in the twilight—and they did not cross the river."

Shannon pondered this for a moment.

"I'm not too familiar with this part of the country," he said, "but if I remember correctly there's a town a few miles downriver from here. I've forgotten the name."

"Ah, yes," Ramón said slowly. "A place named Casa Cochina. It is a very rough town, like most settlements along the Pecos. Do you think some of the *banditos* may have gone there?"

Shannon stood up.

"I don't know," he said, "but I'm going to find out. Do you think you can bear to spend another hour in the saddle?"

Ramón laughed.

"*Patrón,*" he said, "I have spent forty years in the saddle. One more hour will make no difference."

"Good," Shannon said. "Then let's pay a call on this Casa Cochina."

## Chapter Five

The vaqueros all wanted to go with them, but Shannon vetoed the idea.

"We need someone to remain here in case any of the rustlers try to cross back over the river during the night," he said. "Ramón, pick two men to come with us. The others can rest here while we're gone. Tell them we'll be back by daybreak."

Casa Cochina was five miles downriver from their campsite. As they approached along the riverbank they could see the lights of the town ahead glimmering in the darkness. They could also hear the raucous medley of sounds coming from the streets and buildings—music, shouting, even a few gunshots.

"Looks like an interesting little *pueblo,*" Shannon said

sarcastically as they reached the outskirts. "We may be in for a lively evening."

"As I said," Ramón murmured, "a rough place."

And a rough place it proved to be. Shannon had spent much of his adult life as a lawman in the Kansas cow towns—Dodge, Wichita, Abilene, Caldwell, Ellsworth, and others—so the wildness of Casa Cochina was not unfamiliar to him. Yet as they rode slowly along the main street, he could not help but marvel at what he saw: bright lights, loud noise, people coming and going, laughing and cursing, and the notes of tinny pianos floating out of the saloons, dance halls, and other establishments that lined the walks.

Obviously Casa Cochina was not populated by average, hard-working, God-fearing folk. Drunks staggered along the sidewalks and fell headlong into the streets. Every few yards, it seemed, there was a fight of some sort in progress, and it was evident that the activities going on within the buildings would not have won the approval of the average Eastern clergyman. Probably, Shannon thought, half the people they were passing were already wanted by the law on one side of the Texas border or the other, and the other half soon would be.

"We'll have a hard time spotting any cattle rustlers in all of this," Shannon said to Ramón in disgust. "A few outlaws more or less wouldn't even be noticed here. I wonder if there's a town marshal—he might be able to help us."

He reined in and spoke to a passerby, a gambler by his

attire, and one of the few people they had seen who appeared to be sober.

"Pardon me, friend," Shannon said to him. "Can you tell me where I can find the city marshal's office?"

The man looked sourly up at him.

"Up the street, on the left," he said shortly. He scowled as he saw the U.S. marshal's badge on Shannon's coat.

"Just what we need," he grumbled. "Another blasted lawman. You come to arrest somebody?"

"It's possible," Shannon said mildly.

"Well," said the man with a snicker, "a lot of people here in Casa Cochina don't have much love for the law. If I were you, Marshal, I'd put that tin badge away before somebody decides to use it for a target."

He walked off, glancing over his shoulder as if he were half-expecting Shannon to shoot him in the back.

"Nice fellow," Shannon said. "I can see we're going to make lots of friends here."

He urged the buckskin forward, looking along the street for some indication of a marshal's office.

Ramón rode close beside him, looking around nervously. His eyes were narrowed, and his hand was resting on the butt of his revolver.

"Perhaps that man gave you good advice," he said. "It might be better to hide your badge, or even get off this street entirely."

Shannon shook his head.

"This badge doesn't hide," he said. "And neither do I."

Ramón sighed at this declaration of folly, but he knew

Shannon well enough to know that he meant exactly what he said, so he did not offer any further protest.

They found the city marshal's office in the next block. Shannon tied his horse to the hitchrail. "Stay here with the others, Ramón," he said. "I'll see what I can find out."

He stepped onto the boardwalk, moving toward the open door of the office. As he approached the doorway, two men who had been sitting outside it rose from their chairs and blocked his path. Both wore stars on their shirts, and one of them was holding a shotgun which he pointed at Shannon's midsection.

"Whaddaya want, mister?" asked the man with the shotgun.

"I'd like to see the marshal," Shannon replied. "Would that be either of you?"

"No," said the other man. "Why do you want to see him?"

"Business," Shannon said. "Just business."

The man with the shotgun had now caught sight of the badge on Shannon's coat.

"Say," he said, "are you a lawman?"

"U.S. marshal," Shannon replied. "All right if I go inside?"

"Oh, yeah, sure," said the deputy, moving aside to let him pass. "Sorry, Marshal, I didn't see the badge at first. We got to be careful in this town if we want to live very long."

Shannon stepped through the doorway into the office. The gray-haired man sitting at the desk looked up sharply at Shannon as he entered. Then he rose from his chair and came forward, his hand extended and a broad smile on his face.

"Clay Shannon!" he said. "As I live and breathe! I haven't laid eyes on you since Wichita."

Shannon stiffened momentarily, then relaxed as he recognized the man. The marshal of Casa Cochina was an old acquaintance, Pat Casey, with whom he had served as deputy marshal in one of the Kansas trail towns in the days of the Texas cattle drives. Shannon laughed and shook Casey's proffered hand.

"Hello, Pat," he said. "I never expected to see a friendly face in this owlhoot's paradise."

Casey grinned.

"Awful, isn't it?" he said. "The last stop on the road to perdition."

He waved Shannon to a chair and poured him a cup of coffee from a pot that stood on the nearby woodstove.

"How long have you been marshaling here?" Shannon asked. "I thought you'd retired years ago."

"A man's got to eat," Casey said, "and now that the days of the big cattle drives are over, the cities up north don't have much use for an old town-tamer anymore. But what about you? I see by the tin on your chest that you're a U.S. marshal now. What brings you to this sinkhole? Nobody comes here for their health."

Shannon briefly described his odyssey from Kansas lawman to New Mexico rancher, then explained the circumstances that had brought him to Casa Cochina.

When he had finished, Casey gave a low whistle.

"Two thousand head, you say? That's a lot of beef. And you think they're driving the herd to Texas?"

"Yes," said Shannon. "They've crossed the Pecos, and there's not much ahead of them this side of the Texas line. I've got some men guarding the crossing upriver, and we think that most of the rustlers went on across with the herd, but it looks like three or four of the gang decided to ride into town for some amusement before moving on. We tracked them here from the spot where the herd was taken across the river."

"Three or four of them, eh?" Casey said, putting down his coffee cup. "Any idea what they look like?"

"Not a clue," Shannon replied. "I'd hoped you might have noticed strangers in town tonight, but I can see that a few cattle rustlers would blend right into the crowd here."

"That's true," Casey said, rubbing his chin thoughtfully, "but you just may be in luck. Believe it or not, we keep a pretty close eye on the chaos out there. We don't do much about it, because nobody wants us to, but we try to take note when new faces hit town so we know what kind of trouble to expect next."

Shannon's eyebrows went up.

"You mean you've seen someone ride in recently who might be part of this gang?"

"It's possible. We picked up two characters earlier today who looked like they might have been punching cows recently. Smelled like it too. They rode in from upriver this morning, bought some supplies, then headed for the saloons. They were getting a bit too frisky in one of the joints, so we stuck 'em in the hoosegow for a couple of hours to let 'em sober up. A third man came and bailed them out just a little while ago. We let people do that here—bail their friends out, I mean. The jail isn't big enough to hold every drunk in town, and we figure if they spend their money on bail they'll have less to spend on liquor."

"Just three?" Shannon said doubtfully. "From the hoofprints we were following, it looked as if there might be four of them."

"Only saw three," Casey said. "Sorry."

"Who were they?" Shannon asked. "Did you find out their names?"

"Don't know who the drunks were," Casey said, "but the man who bailed them out gave his name. Said it was, um, Snyder. Yeah, that was it. Snyder."

Shannon thought for a moment. One of the men he had run out of Los Santos a year earlier had been named Snyder. Shannon had fought with him in a livery stable after Snyder had participated in the beating of the old man who was serving as the sheriff of Los Santos. Could it be the same person? The dead man they had found on the trail the day before, Finch, had been one of the same crowd.

"I may know him," Shannon said. He told Casey of the incident in Los Santos and the discovery of the deceased Finch.

Casey shook his head.

"You must live right, Clay," he marveled. "Like I said,

we just turned 'em loose a little while ago. They may still be in town."

He got up and retrieved his hat from a peg by the door.

"Let's go see what we can find," he said. "I'm a tolerant man, but I never did cotton to cattle rustlers much. Especially ones who kill honest ranch hands while they're doing the rustling."

## Chapter Six

Followed at a respectful distance by the two town deputies, Shannon and Marshal Casey began checking Casa Cochina's saloons, hoping to catch sight of the men of whom Casey had spoken. In each saloon they entered, people glared belligerently at the town marshal and then turned equally dark scowls upon Shannon. Clearly, the majority of the citizens of Casa Cochina shared the opinion of the gambler to whom Shannon had spoken earlier that the town was not in need of any additional lawmen.

The third saloon they tried was named "Pecos Rest." There was, in fact, nothing restful about it, for it was a large place filled with sweaty men, cigar smoke, the smell of cheap whiskey, and the hubbub of many drunken voices. A man in a derby hat and sleeve garters was pounding away vigorously on a battered piano, adding its off-key notes to the general bedlam.

As Shannon and Casey were surveying the room, a large, bearded man pushed himself out of his chair and, holding a half-full whiskey bottle by the neck, lurched toward the two lawmen.

"Whatcha want in here, Casey?" the man growled. "You ain't welcome here, and you know it."

The man was a head taller than either of the two lawmen, and he loomed over them menacingly, his eyes red and wild.

Marshal Casey regarded him coldly.

"Sit down, Pete," he said. "I've warned you before to behave yourself. If you give me any trouble, you'll spend the night in the drunk tank instead of here with that whiskey bottle."

The man's face darkened and his eyes bulged.

"Oh, yeah?" he bellowed. "We'll see about that. I've had all I'm gonna take from you, law dog. This time I'll gut you like a fish!"

He smashed the whiskey bottle on the edge of the nearest table, and then, holding the jagged remains before him, lunged at Casey. Before Casey could move, Shannon had drawn his six-gun and slammed it hard against the man's temple. Pete went down like a butchered steer and lay moaning in a puddle of liquor and shards of glass from the broken bottle.

Casey regarded the buffaloed drunk for a moment and then looked admiringly at Shannon.

"Well, I see you haven't slowed down any, Clay," he said. "I remember you doing that to a couple of trouble-makers in Wichita, and I guess being a rich cattle baron hasn't spoiled your technique a bit."

Shannon reholstered his revolver.

"What'll we do with him?" he said, indicating the insensible figure stretched out on the floor.

"The boys will take care of him," Casey said, motioning for the two town deputies who had followed them into the saloon to pick up the drunk and carry him out.

"Well, I guess your birds aren't here," Casey went on. "Let's try the River House across the street."

"Wait a minute," Shannon said, putting his hand on Casey's arm. "Look."

At the far end of the room, a man had gotten up from a table and was sidling out the rear door, keeping his face turned away from the two marshals.

"Look familiar?" Shannon asked.

"Yeah," Casey said, peering through the thick atmosphere of the room. "That's the guy who bailed out the other two today. Snyder."

"Come on," Shannon said. "Let's follow him. He may lead us to the others. I want all of them."

They hurried back out to the street and moved around the corner toward the rear of Pecos Rest. The figure of a man could just be seen making his way quickly away from the saloon. Shannon and Casey followed, keeping a discreet distance behind and staying in the shadows as they passed between the lamplit buildings.

They drew back against a wall out of sight as, a hundred yards further on, the object of their attention paused outside a livery stable. He glanced anxiously back up the street, then went into the stable.

"Well, well," Casey said. "Looks like he's planning a little trip."

"Let's see if we can change his plans," Shannon replied, starting forward again.

They moved apart as they approached the stable, each taking one side of the open stable door. Shannon peered around the door and saw that three men, one of them Snyder, were in the stalls saddling horses in great haste.

Shannon slipped the rawhide loop off the hammer of his Colt and then stepped inside.

"Well, Snyder," he said calmly, "it seems that you and I are destined to meet only in livery stables. Step away from that horse and keep your hands where I can see them."

All three men froze in surprise.

"Shannon!" Snyder exclaimed.

"The very same," Shannon said, resting his hand on the ivory grips of his revolver. "Move away from those horses, all of you, and come out here into the light. And when you move, do it very carefully. Now let's go—I won't tell you again."

The three men reluctantly came out of the stalls and stood in the center of the stable, eyeing Shannon and Marshal Casey nervously.

"What's this, Marshal?" Snyder said to Casey. "We paid our bail, and we're leavin' nice and peaceful."

"The bail's revoked, Snyder," Shannon said. "And you've got a lot more to worry about now than a charge of public drunkeness. You're under arrest for cattle theft and murder. Undo those gunbelts and put them on the floor. Do it very slowly, because I'd like nothing better than to have an excuse to blow your ugly heads off."

The men hesitated, glancing at one another. For a moment, it seemed as if they would surrender. Then they tensed, their eyes riveted on the lawmen, and Shannon's heart sank as he saw that they were going to make a fight of it. Three against two. He shouldn't have dragged Casey into it.

"Don't do it, Snyder," he said loudly. "I want you alive, but I'll take you dead if I have to."

Snyder cursed and went for his six-gun. The other two men followed suit, a split second behind Snyder. But Snyder's companions were quicker on the draw than he was. He was still trying to drag his revolver out of his holster when the other men cleared leather. Shannon's Colt was in his hand, bucking as he thumbed the hammer twice. The sound of the explosions was earsplitting in the confines of the stable. The two gunmen went over backwards and lay in twisted heaps, their weapons bouncing into the straw beside them. Snyder froze, his six-gun out of the holster but still uncocked as he stared in disbelief at his two fallen companions.

"Give it up, Snyder," Shannon said, centering his revolver barrel on Snyder's stomach. "Last chance."

From behind Shannon and Casey, the sound of another

gunshot exploded through the livery stable. Casey grunted and spun away to his right. Even as Shannon whirled to meet the new threat, a second shot shattered the night beyond the stable door, and a bullet whipped past Shannon's ear. It smashed the oil lamp hanging in the center of the stable, bringing the lamp to the floor. The lamp oil splashed out onto the straw, setting it afire.

Both lawmen fired blindly several times into the street. They were rewarded by a loud scream from the darkness.

"Watch the street!" Shannon called to Casey, who was on his knees facing the door. "I'll get Snyder!"

But Snyder had taken advantage of the opportunity created by the distraction. Shannon turned back toward the interior of the stable just in time to see the outlaw throw himself onto his horse and spur the animal forward toward him. Shannon raised his pistol to fire, but the hammer fell on an empty chamber. Thwarted, Shannon could only fling himself aside to avoid being trampled as the frightened horse with Snyder aboard lunged past him.

"Get him, Pat!" Shannon shouted. Casey fired once at Snyder's back, and then horse and rider were swallowed up in the night.

Cursing roundly under his breath, Shannon grabbed a saddle blanket and smothered the flames from the fallen oil lamp. A second lamp stood on a shelf nearby, and Shannon, still half-blinded by the recent gunflashes, fumbled through the dark to find and light it. Adjusting the wick, he held it up and looked around.

Casey was just getting to his feet. He had holstered his

revolver and was holding the upper part of his left arm.

"Are you all right?" Shannon asked anxiously, hurrying over to him.

"Yeah, I'm fine," Casey replied. "Whoever it was just nicked me. I've cut myself worse shaving." He looked out the stable door at the street.

"I guess there were four of 'em after all," he said ruefully. "I never was much good at arithmetic."

"Well, we found the fourth one," said Shannon. "Or rather, he found us." He started toward the door. "Come on," he said. "One of us must have hit him—I heard him yell."

They discovered the fourth man lying against the wall of the building opposite the livery stable. Shannon held up the lamp. The man appeared to be Mexican, and he was clutching at a gaping wound in his chest.

Casey's two deputies came running up, guns drawn. Ramón was with them, as were the other two Alvarez vaqueros.

"Get the doc," Casey said to the deputies.

Shannon crouched down beside the injured man.

"Where are your gang taking the cattle?" he demanded.

"I know nothing about any cattle," the man wheezed. "Get a priest—I must make my confession."

"Make your confession to me," Shannon said harshly. "Snyder's run off and left you. You don't owe him anything. So tell me—where are they taking the cattle?"

The man was coughing now, struggling to get his breath.

"I do not know any 'Snyder,' " he said thickly. "Let me alone."

A tall man carrying a medical bag hurried up and elbowed Shannon aside.

"Give me some light, there," he snapped. Shannon held up the lamp he was carrying. The doctor examined the wound, then pressed his stethoscope against the man's heaving chest.

"How bad is he?" Casey said. The doctor took off the stethoscope, folded it carefully, and put it back in his bag.

"Did he ask for a priest?" he said, looking up at Casey and Shannon.

"Yes," Shannon said.

"Well," said the doctor, "you'd better get one—fast."

The priest arrived within minutes.

"Leave us," he said to the men who had gathered at the scene. "I must hear his confession."

"I want to question him," Shannon said.

"He has no time for questions now," the priest said. "Stand back."

He bent over the dying man to hear his confession. Shannon and the others moved away. Shannon watched for a moment, then moved quietly forward again until he could hear what was being said.

"Forgive me, Father, for I have sinned," the dying gunman murmured. "I have killed men. I have stolen cattle. I have. . . "

"Where were you taking the cattle, my son?" Shannon

asked in a low voice. The priest twisted around and glared at him, his mouth open to utter a reproof.

"We were taking them to Texas, Father," the man whispered. "To sell them to the *gringo* army. Oh, Father, I am heartily sorry for my misdeeds. . . ."

His voice trailed off and his breathing ceased.

The priest was on his feet now, his eyes angry as he faced Shannon.

"The confessional is sacred," said the priest. "It was wrong of you to listen. Have you no shame?"

"It's also wrong to steal cattle and kill men, Father," Shannon said dryly. "If there's any shame, it's his, not mine."

"May God forgive you," said the priest, shaking his head.

"I hope He will, Father," Shannon replied in a weary voice. "I have a lot to be forgiven for."


They searched the dead man's clothing. In his pocket they found a silver crucifix, worn and tarnished with age and long use.

"Ramón," Shannon said, holding out the crucifix, "this looks familiar. Have you ever seen it before?" Ramón took the crucifix and looked closely at it in the lamplight.

"Truly," he said. "It belonged to Miguel, one of the men the rustlers killed. I have seen him with it many times."

"Keep it, then," Shannon said, "and give it to Miguel's widow. At least she'll have something to remember him by."

He got to his feet.

"Now," he said to Ramón and the vaqueros, "let's get moving. It'll be almost daylight by the time we arrive back at the crossing, and I want to get started after the cattle and our friend Snyder."

Marshal Casey was standing nearby, watching. Before departing, the doctor had bandaged his arm.

"I'm sorry about Snyder, Clay," Casey said as Shannon arose. "I had a clear shot at him when he was riding out of the stable door, and I missed. Guess I'm getting old."

"Don't worry about it, Pat," Shannon said. "It's my fault. I should have killed Snyder a year ago in Los Santos, when I had the chance. I won't make the same mistake again."

## Chapter Seven

Dawn was breaking as they reached their camp on the riverbank. The men listened intently as Ramón related to them all that had happened in Casa Cochina. When he took out Miguel's crucifix and held it up for them to see, they gave a low growl and stirred uneasily.

"Vengeance for Miguel!" shouted one, and the others took up the cry.

Shannon held up his hand.

"Hold it," he said, listening. "I think we're about to have company."

The sound of horses approaching from the northwest sent them all scurrying for cover, and the clatter of repeating rifles being cocked filled the air. Then, as they watched warily, a dozen riders came into view over the rise that led down to the camp on the riverbank.

"It's all right," Shannon said. "It's our own people."

The vaqueros from Rancho Alvarez rode down the slope, reined in, and dismounted amid general shouts of welcome.

"Good," Shannon said, when the greetings had died down. "Now we can. . . ."

Ramón was still watching the top of the rise.

"Señor Shannon," he said with a smile, "we have another visitor, I think."

Shannon sighed. He knew without looking who the new arrival would be.

Charlotte brought her horse down to the river at a slow walk and pulled up in front of Shannon.

"Surprised?" she said with a mischievous smile.

"No," Shannon said sourly. "I knew it was only a matter of time." He shook his head, remembering the night long ago when he had ridden into Los Santos to face down the outlaws who had taken over the town. He had ordered Charlotte to stay behind at the ranch then too, but stubbornly she had followed him, arriving just in time to put a bullet in the gunman who was about to draw on Shannon.

"One of these days I'm going to stop leaving you behind," he said. "It doesn't do a bit of good."

Charlotte laughed, then dismounted and moved closer to him.

"You're not angry, then?" she said, looking up at him with a hopeful smile.

"Yes, I am," Shannon said. "Oh well—no, I'm not. Anyway, you're here. Have you had any breakfast?"

They ate rapidly, swallowing the cold beans without

really tasting them. Everyone was anxious to cross the river and resume the pursuit.

"I'll send someone across to see if anybody is lying in wait for us over there," Ramón said, studying the opposite bank of the river.

"No," Shannon said. "That's my job. I'll go across first, by myself. If anyone is waiting over there to drygulch us, I don't want to put our men in the middle of the river for them to shoot at. Wait here, all of you."

He climbed aboard the buckskin and started into the river. Charlotte remounted and followed him. Shannon reined up and pointed back to the bank.

"Not this time, *esposa mia,*" Shannon said. "I mean it. Go back and wait for me. Please."

"I'm not afraid," Charlotte said, drawing up beside him.

"It isn't a matter of being afraid," said Shannon irritably. "Hunting men is my profession, Charlotte. Let me do my job as I see fit."

Charlotte started to say that she thought that ranching was now his profession, then thought better of it. She knew that Clay Shannon was a lawman, first and last, and she was wise enough to know that she would never change him. She leaned over and kissed him on the cheek, then turned her horse around.

"Be careful, Marshal," she said, and rode back to the bank where the vaqueros waited.

Shannon slid his Winchester out of its saddle scabbard, levered a cartridge into the chamber, and then, holding the cocked rifle at the ready, turned his horse toward the opposite shore. The river at this point was shallow, but he went carefully, anticipating the possibility of quicksand. Knowing that the buckskin would be a better judge of the footing than he, Shannon let the animal pick its own way through the water while he surveyed the rocks on the opposite bank. The sun was well up now, and, as he was headed for the east bank of the Pecos, the sunlight was in his eyes. *I'm breaking one of the rules,* he thought. Long ago his mentor, a veteran lawman, had taught him that, if faced with a possible gunfight, it was always best to approach your opponents with the sun at your back. *That way,* the old gunfighter had said, *it will shine in your enemies' eyes, not yours.*

But now he had no choice, for his course lay to the east—almost directly into the sun—and the glare was making it difficult for him to see what might be lurking in the shadows beyond.

His apprehension grew as he neared the middle of the river. Would the rustlers have left men behind to ambush them? It was likely, and, as he had told Ramón earlier, this was an ideal spot for it. Besides, shooting someone from cover would be exactly Snyder's style.

He brought the buckskin to an abrupt halt. Something— instinct, sixth sense, or perhaps just long experience—told him that he was riding into great danger. He knew that he should turn back, take the men upstream or downstream, find another crossing, and pick up the trail of the cattle later. But that would mean a delay of many hours, and, more importantly, it would mean turning tail and retreating from peril in full view of his wife and the men he led, and that he could not bring himself to do.

*I'm just like everybody else,* he thought. *I'd rather die than make a fool of myself.*

Cursing himself for having started into the river to begin with, he lifted the reins to urge the buckskin forward. At that moment, confirmation of his suspicions arrived in a most emphatic fashion. Smoke spurted from among the rocks, and the crack of rifles reached him just as a welter of splashes on the surface of the river around him told him that he was under fire. Confronted with this sudden threat, most men would have wheeled their mounts and fled back to the safety of the shore, but Shannon was not like most men. All his life, when faced with trouble or danger, his instinctive reaction had been to go forward, to attack, to overwhelm and defeat the peril and those creating it. This trait had often gotten him into trouble—a fact that, in his more introspective moments, he recognized clearly—but for better or worse, it was his nature to confront a problem or an enemy head-on, and this moment was no exception. He kicked the buckskin's sides and the animal leapt forward as Shannon drove him toward the sound of the guns.

But the horse had taken scarcely two leaps when it suddenly pitched forward and fell. As the stallion went down, Shannon was thrown over its neck and into the river. Stunned, Shannon lay for a moment in the muddy water, trying to get his bearings. His first thought was for the horse—had it been shot? The memory of another much-loved buckskin horse, deliberately killed by a brutal enemy years ago, flashed through his mind.

*Not again,* he thought. *Please, not again.*

But the horse was scrambling to its feet, shaking itself as it rose from the water.

*Not hit,* Shannon thought with relief. *Stumbled. Not hit.*

But, although neither horse nor rider had yet been struck by a bullet, it was apparent that this would inevitably happen, and soon, for as he got to his hands and knees the sound of gunfire from the opposite shore intensified, and the little jets of water began to leap up around him in greater numbers. He grabbed the buckskin's reins and started to lead it hurriedly back to the western bank of the river, but even as he turned he saw that Charlotte had spurred her horse forward into the water and was riding hard toward him.

"Go back!" Shannon shouted. "Go back! I'm all right!"

But she paid no heed, urging the horse through the shallows toward Shannon. The vaqueros, who had been shooting at the opposite shore to give Shannon cover, now hastily mounted their horses and galloped headlong into the river, shouting loudly and firing at the distant gunflashes.

"I'm coming, Clay!" Charlotte called, ignoring Shannon's frantic shouts and gestures. At first, it seemed that she would reach him without being hit, but then, when she was barely ten yards away, her body jerked convulsively as if from a heavy blow, and with a loud cry she pitched out of the saddle and went headlong into the water.

Icy fear gripped Shannon, a fear greater, perhaps, than

any he had ever known. He dropped the buckskin's reins and splashed through the water toward his fallen bride. Charlotte was writhing in pain in the shallows, and Shannon's heart nearly stopped as he saw that the river around her was tinged with red. Desperately he went to his knees beside her, lifted her in his arms, and staggered toward the riverbank, fighting to keep his footing on the soft bottom. The vaqueros, enraged to see their mistress fall, charged past Shannon, firing rapidly at the enemy. Ramón was beside Shannon now, and together, under cover of the vaqueros counterfire, they brought Charlotte to shore. They laid her gently in the shelter of a large boulder, and Shannon slipped a folded saddle blanket under her head.

"How bad is it?" Ramón asked anxiously, bending over her.

"Bad enough," Shannon said. "Get the vaqueros back here, Ramón, while I attend to her. They'll be slaughtered out there in the open river."

Ramón leapt back into the saddle and rode to the water's edge, bellowing at the Alvarez men to return. Reluctantly, they obeyed, firing a few parting shots as they turned their horses. Two of them had been wounded by the gunfire, but they remained in their saddles and made it safely back to dry land.

Shannon cut away the lower portion of Charlotte's bloodstained shirt so that he could see the bullet hole. The slug had passed through her side and exited out her back. The wound was bleeding profusely, and she was now unconscious.

Rage boiled through Shannon. He wanted desperately to stay with Charlotte, but they were still under fire and there was insufficient cover on their side of the river to protect all of their men and animals. He had to act quickly.

The riderless buckskin had followed him out of the river, and Shannon snatched a clean shirt from his saddlebags. Working in feverish haste, he tore the shirt into strips and knelt beside Charlotte to bind up her wound. Then he leapt to his feet again.

"Esteban!" he said to one of the waiting vaqueros. "Stay here with her. Care for her until I return!"

He caught up the buckskin's reins and climbed into the saddle. The other vaqueros crowded around him.

"How is it with Doña Carlota?" one of them asked him anxiously, using Charlotte's Spanish name. Through the red mist of his anger, Shannon saw the concern in their faces, and was touched by it.

"She's badly injured," he said. "I fear for her."

A shout of protest went up among the vaqueros.

"Those who harmed her will pay for it with their lives," Ramón said fiercely. "I swear it!" The vaqueros roared their agreement. Several of them sheathed their rifles and drew their knives.

"Are you ready, *amigos?*" Shannon called out, drawing his six-gun. "Then—follow me!"

They whipped their horses around and plunged together into the river, spreading out as they rode, each of them straining to be the first to reach the other side. Heedless of the hostile gunfire, they charged headlong through the shallow water, sending sheets of spray high into the air as they thundered toward the far shore.

Riding in the forefront of the pack, Shannon, through his grief and wrath, felt a sense of wonder at the terrible power of the charge. His heart raced and his breath came in gasps as the avenging vaqueros surged around him, and the madness of their apocalyptic ride filled his very soul with a fierce exhilaration unlike anything he had ever felt before. In the frenzy of the moment, all danger was forgotten; he wanted only to find and kill the cowardly assassins who had shot down his wife in cold blood as she came to help him.

On they rode, across the seemingly endless river. A vaquero went down, struck by a bullet, and then another. Then at last they were across, racing toward the rocks that sheltered their assailants. A man rose up almost under the buckskin's hooves, aiming a rifle at Shannon. Shannon shot him between the eyes. Two more men broke from cover, fleeing in panic toward their tethered horses as the irresistible force of the vaqueros' charge came rushing toward them. They went down screaming beneath the hooves of the oncoming riders. Another outlaw made it to his horse and clawed his way into the saddle, firing back at them with his six-gun as they came. One of his shots struck home, and yet another of the vaqueros went down. A new surge of fury washed over Shannon, and he rammed the plunging buckskin's chest hard against the flank of the outlaw's mount. Horse and rider went down heavily. The bandit scrambled to his feet as Shannon loomed above him on the rearing horse. Casting away his revolver, the man, now nearly mad with terror, stretched out his hands in supplication, begging for mercy. The Colt bucked in Shannon's hand, and the man reeled backwards, dead before his body hit the ground.

Shannon looked around for other targets, but even as he did so he saw that the fight was over. The last shots of the battle were already echoing away into the rocks as the vaqueros slid from their saddles and converged near the fallen outlaws.

The red mist was at last beginning to clear from Shannon's brain, and he stared with sudden shock at the body of the man who had begged for his life even as Shannon gunned him down. *Did I really do that?* Shannon thought to himself. *What came over me? I never shot an unarmed man before in my whole life.* He shuddered, ashamed at what he had just done. *Now I'm no better than they are,* he thought sadly.

Ramón walked over to him, slipping fresh cartridges into the magazine of his rifle.

"The señora has been avenged," he said with satisfaction. "The *banditos* have paid for their evil deeds."

"Did any of them get away?" Shannon asked, trying to gather his thoughts into some semblance of order.

"No," Ramón said. "One of them was still alive when we found him, but I think that he is almost certainly dead by now. The vaqueros were very angry with him." Shannon nodded, trying not to feel pity for the man who had been unwise enough not to die immediately.

## Chapter Eight

Without waiting for the rest of the vaqueros, Shannon sent the buckskin plunging into the river once more and crossed back to the place on the far side where he had left Charlotte. Esteban was sitting next to her, bathing her forehead with a wet neckerchief. Charlotte was conscious now, but her face was pale and it was obvious that she was in great pain.

"Are you all right, Clay?" she asked as he knelt beside her.

"I'm fine," he said gruffly. "The question is, how are you?"

"It's nothing," she said in a weak voice. "Just a scratch. Did you get them?"

"We got them," Shannon said, trying not to think of the man who had begged him for mercy.

"And the cattle?" Charlotte said, struggling to sit up.

Shannon eased her back to the ground.

"They're gone," he said. "It looks like the rustlers are still driving them southeastward."

"Then go after them, Clay," she cried. "*Find them*. I want our herd back. Don't worry about me—I'll be all right."

"Of course you will," Shannon said, forcing a smile. He rose and took Ramón aside, out of Charlotte's hearing.

"We have to get her to town," he said. "They've got a doctor there. She can't ride, so we'll have to make something for her to lie on while we carry her."

Ramón nodded.

"There are a few trees further downstream along the bank of the river," he said. "I will make a travois as *los Indios* do. It will be hard for her, but it will be the quickest way."

"Thank you, my friend," Shannon said. "You've done well today." Then he remembered that others besides Charlotte had been hurt in the attack.

"I saw several vaqueros go down," he said. "Was anyone killed?"

"No, Señor, *gracias a Dios*. But three of them are seriously wounded, and two more are injured badly enough to need a doctor's attention."

"Very well. We'll take them to Casa Cochina along with Doña Carlota."

"Shall we send some men after the herd?"

"No," Shannon said. "We'll need nearly everyone's help getting the injured into town, and besides, I don't want to send just a few men up against those killers. The herd will have to wait."

"But the *banditos* will escape," said Ramón, frowning.

"No they won't," Shannon said grimly. "They will *not* escape. That I promise you. We'll follow them when we can, and we'll find them, no matter where they've gone."

*"Bueno!"* said Ramón. "I will tell the men."

They reached Casa Cochina shortly before noon. The journey had been slow and rough, causing great discomfort to Charlotte and the injured vaqueros. At that hour the town was relatively quiet, but people began coming out onto the street to gape at them as they rode by. When they reached the marshal's office, Pat Casey and his two deputies appeared. Casey had a bandage on his arm, a souvenir of the fight in the livery stable the night before.

"Good grief, Clay," Casey said, gazing in wonder at the procession. "It looks like your private army has been busy this morning. And who's the pretty lady? Looks like she's a casualty too."

"This is no joking matter, Pat," Shannon said, tying his horse to the hitch rail in front of the office. "Some of these men are hurt, and they need help. As for the 'pretty lady,' she happens to be my wife, and she's badly wounded also. Have somebody get the doctor, will you?"

"He's on the way," Casey said. "I sent for him when I saw you coming. I'm sorry about your wife and your men—I didn't mean to make light of it. You've obviously had a bad time."

"Not nearly as bad a time as the people who did it will have when I catch up with them," Shannon said.

The doctor appeared and began checking the wounded.

"Move them over to my office," he ordered. "Take the woman first. Get her into the back room behind the office and put her into the bed. Hurry."

While the doctor ministered to Charlotte and the others, Shannon explained to Casey what had occurred.

"You're still going to chase them?" Casey asked skeptically.

"Yes," Shannon replied. "And I'll get them too."

"What about your wife?"

"Look after her for me, Pat—please. Make sure she's cared for day and night until she's out of danger. She's as stubborn as a mule, and it won't be long before she'll try to get up and follow us. Don't let her. Handcuff her to the bed if you have to, but keep her here until I get back. I don't want to lose her."

His voice broke as he said it, and Casey looked at him sharply.

"Sounds like you're kinda fond of her," he said with a grin.

"More than you can ever imagine," said Shannon gruffly, looking away.

"Well," Casey said, "if she's as stubborn as she is good looking, she'll be a handful. But don't worry, I'll take good care of her. You can count on it."

"Thanks, Pat. I won't forget your kindness."

"No thanks needed," Casey replied. "Those were great days we spent together in Wichita, and as I recall, you saved my bacon a couple of times when things got hot. I'm glad to have the chance to help you now. But be careful, *amigo*. From the sound of it, you're up against a pretty rugged bunch, and with some of your men out of action, you'll be bucking the odds when you catch up to them. I wish I could spare my deputies to ride along with you, but we've got all we can do to keep the lid on here."

"That's all right, Pat," Shannon said. "Thanks anyway. We'll manage."

At length the doctor came out of the room where Charlotte lay.

"You can go in now," he said to Shannon. "But don't stay too long."

"How is she?" Shannon asked anxiously.

The doctor shrugged.

"The bullet grazed a rib and went through cleanly. Nothing vital was hit. But she's weak from loss of blood, and the pain will be bad for awhile. I've given her some laudanum to make her more comfortable."

Charlotte lay quietly in the bed, her dark hair spread out upon the pillow. She gave Shannon a weak smile as he came into the room and sat down in the chair beside her.

"I'm sorry about this, Clay," she said. "But don't let me delay you. You *are* going after them, aren't you?"

Shannon nodded.

"As soon as I'm certain that you and the wounded vaqueros are properly taken care of, we'll be moving out."

"Good," she said. "When I'm able, I'll follow you."

"You'll stay here until I get back, lady, and no arguments," Shannon replied quickly. "The marshal here is a fellow named Pat Casey. He's a good lawman and an old friend of mine. He'll look after you until I get back. And the doctor's wife will be here too, so you'll be well cared for. I'll also leave two or three of our own men behind, just in case."

Charlotte reached out her hand and clasped his tightly.

"Be careful, marshal of mine," she said. "You're more important to me than all the cattle in the world."

Shannon laughed.

"I'll try to arrange for you to have both," he said. "In the meantime, you need rest, so go to sleep now. I'll stay here with you for awhile."

He sat with her for a time, holding her hand. At length the laudanum did its work, and she drifted off to sleep. Shannon rose quietly and then stood beside the bed for a moment, looking down at her. The madness that had filled him during the fight at the river had faded now, but a fierce determination had taken its place. He had lost much in his lifetime—his mother had died when he was a child, and his father, the marshal of a little Kansas town, had been shot down trying to arrest a drunken killer. Then his first wife, Kathy, and their little son had been taken from him— they now lay in untended graves in a ghost town far to the north. After the death of his family, Shannon had made a new start in New Mexico, fighting for Rancho Alvarez and the Alvarez family against the evil men who would have destroyed them both. Now Rancho Alvarez was his home, and Charlotte Alvarez his wife. Yet once again evil men were trying to take her from him, and those men must be destroyed—not merely because they had stolen his property and harmed his wife, but, just as importantly, because they had set themselves above the law. They had stolen and killed, and he must see that they stole and killed no more. The badge he wore demanded no less. That was Shannon's way. It always had been, and it always would be.

Charlotte moved restlessly in her sleep. Her face was as pale as the pillow she lay upon, and from time to time, even in her sleep, she moaned softly.

As he watched her moving restlessly in her pain, Shannon's fury grew white-hot, filling his heart with a fierce desire for retribution.

*I'll get them, Charlotte,* he whispered as he gazed down at her. *I'll get them for you. For you and for me and for our dead and for the law. I swear it.*

He slipped quietly out of the room, on his way to keep his vow.

## Chapter Nine

They forded the Pecos near Casa Cochina and followed the southeast bank downstream to the place where the cattle had been taken across. The tracks of their stolen herd stretched away from the river, heading unswervingly southeast.

It was hotter here than it had been further north, and soon men and horses were sweating uncomfortably. The vaqueros began shedding their coats, and Shannon soon followed suit, remembering first, however, to unpin the U.S. marshal's badge from his coat and repin it securely above the pocket of his shirt.

The country through which they were traveling was flatter than that which they had just left, for east of the Pecos began the Llano Estacado, the famous Staked Plain of the Southwest. Although the hills were far lower than they had been west of the river, the land was still rough and broken, cut here and there by great gullies and dry washes that made progress slow and would provide excellent cover for another ambush.

"They must have a definite destination in mind," Shannon said to Ramón as they followed the trail up out of a dry riverbed and back onto high ground. "They keep going in the same direction, regardless of the land and regardless of us."

"Soon they will be in Texas," Ramón said. "Whatever they have in mind, it lies there."

"It looks like it," Shannon mused. "But they could still turn south at any time and cross the Rio Grande into Mexico. If we knew where they were headed, we might be able to cut across country and get ahead of them, instead of just following along like this. How far behind them would you say we are?"

Ramón leaned out of the saddle and inspected the tracks.

"A day at least," he said. "I fear we will not catch them by nightfall."

Shannon glanced back at the sun now sinking toward the western horizon behind them. He still did not want to risk stumbling upon a superior foe in the dark, but the thought of stopping again and losing many hours waiting for another dawn was unacceptable to him.

"We'll rest for an hour after sundown, then go on," he said. "I know it's risky, but with a good moon and a little luck, we'll see them or hear them before they know we're close."

Ramón looked doubtful.

"They will have riders trailing behind to watch for us, will they not?"

"Yes," Shannon said. "And I'll be up ahead watching for them."

They stopped briefly as night fell to rest the horses and take a few bites of food. Then they were back in the saddle, resuming their pursuit. No one complained, for they were proud men who craved vengeance for their comrades and for their wounded mistress. The slight discomfort of a night march meant little to them.

Shannon rode well out in front of them, staying away from the tracks of the cattle and watching the darkness ahead for any sign of danger.

The moon rose, providing the illumination that Shannon had hoped for, but to his dismay it was not long before lightning began flickering on the horizon. As the flashes intensified and the rumble of thunder grew louder, it became apparent that the storm was coming steadily closer. Long before midnight gigantic thunderheads were towering overhead and the moon soon vanished behind them, as if fleeing from the awesome display of electricity that now filled the night.

With the disappearance of the moon and the spread of the thunderclouds across the sky, thick darkness descended upon Shannon and his men, a darkness so profound that it was impossible to see the cattle tracks without dismounting and literally feeling for the impressions in the earth. Only in the glare of the lightning flashes could the trail still be discerned from the back of a horse.

Then it began to rain.

Shannon pulled his slicker from behind his saddle and donned it awkwardly as he rode, muttering under his breath, into the teeth of the storm. The buckskin, made edgy by the rising wind and the rain stinging its face, began to move erratically. Shannon pulled up, debating what to do next.

*I'll bet it doesn't rain three times a year in this country,* Shannon thought. *Why now? Why did it have to be tonight?*

He peered back into the murky darkness looking for the vaqueros who followed. They could easily miss him in the darkness and rain, and then it would be difficult to regain touch with them until the storm passed—however long that might be.

Ramón loomed up through the chaos of the night, guiding his unhappy horse alongside Shannon's.

"Bad luck, this," he shouted against the wind. "The storm will cover the tracks of the cattle. What shall we do?"

A flash of lightning close overhead startled the already jittery horses, and it was several moments before Shannon and Ramón could get them under control again.

"This won't last long," Shannon said. "Not the worst of it, anyway. Meanwhile, we'd better find some shelter. We'll have to stay out of the ravines and dry riverbeds, though. They don't call these storms 'gully-washers' for nothing."

Ramón nodded. It was said that no one familiar with the ways of the Southwest could ever sleep soundly on the sands of a dry riverbed, for fear of the flash floods that could result from a cloudburst just like this one.

"We must keep the vaqueros together," he said, echoing Shannon's earlier thought. "We cannot afford to become separated in the darkness."

They rode back along the trail, seeking the rest of the men, but they found only three. The rest had lost touch in the wildness of the night.

"Come on, let's find cover," Shannon said with disgust. "There's nothing more we can do until this blows over."

They groped their way through the deluge until they found a small cliff with an overhanging ledge. The five men crowded under the ledge's inadequate protection and dismounted to wait out the storm.

"Listen!" Ramón said, tightening his grip on the reins of his nervous horse. "I thought I heard someone shouting."

They strained their ears to catch any sound that might be audible above the rumble of the thunder and the hiss of the heavy rain. Suddenly the high-pitched squealing of a frightened horse could be heard, and then a man began to scream.

"Someone's hurt," Shannon said. "It must be one of our men. He may have fallen, or even ridden over a cliff in the dark."

He mounted the buckskin again, ready to ride back out into the elements. Ramón and the others started to remount as well.

"No, *muchachos,*" Shannon said to them. "I'll go alone. If we all start blundering around out there we'll get separated for sure, and then nobody will be able to find anybody or help anybody. Stay here. If I need you, I'll fire my six-gun to guide you to me. If I'm not back in half an hour, fire your own guns to give me my bearings."

He rode out from under the ledge into the driving rain. The sounds they had heard had come from somewhere to the left of the ledge, so he walked the buckskin in that direction, straining at every step to see what lay before him. The scream came again, this time from closer by.

"Where are you?" Shannon bellowed, trying unsuccessfully to wipe some of the rainwater out of his eyes. "Keep calling. I'll find you."

The next shout seemed to come up out of the ground beneath his feet. Shannon reined in and peered forward. Right in front of him the earth dropped away abruptly into the darkness, and he realized that he had very nearly ridden the buckskin unwittingly over the edge of a deep ravine or dry wash. Shannon swung down from the saddle and, moving carefully, went to the edge of the bluff. Below him, just visible from where he stood, he could see a horse lying on the floor of the dry wash with the body of a man half hidden beneath it.

The man cried out again, and Shannon recognized the voice of Esteban, the vaquero who had ministered to Charlotte beside the Pecos River.

Shannon began to cast about, trying to find a way down the steep slope. The rain had lessened noticeably and the night sky was lightening just enough to restore some visibility, thus aiding him in his search. At length he came upon a break in the cliff and saw a little defile leading down to the floor of the ravine. He started down the incline, leading the buckskin. The way was treacherous, however, and they had gone only a few steps when Shannon felt his boots slipping out from under him. The next moment he found himself sliding uncontrollably down the wet slope. Dropping the reins, he clawed at the earth, trying to slow his descent. Above him, he heard the heavy sound of a horse falling, and he uttered a silent prayer that the buckskin would not roll over him as the two of them went tumbling down.

Then he was at the bottom, winded and bruised but otherwise unhurt. He scrambled up and found himself right beside the buckskin, which was also trying to regain its feet. The horse did not seem to be injured, but it was thoroughly frightened by the experience and tried to dance away from Shannon. Shannon grabbed the reins and soothed the agitated animal.

In the shelter of the ravine walls the wind was hardly noticeable, and the rain had now stopped. Shannon shouted again for Esteban, and was rewarded with an answering call from just a few yards away. Hurrying forward, still leading the buckskin, he found the vaquero lying on the ground, one leg trapped beneath his fallen horse. The animal was struggling to get up but could not do so, and Esteban, still stunned by his fall, was unable to extricate his leg from beneath the horse's side.

Shannon seized the panicked animal's bridle and, after several tries, was able to get it on its feet. In the process he lost his grip on the bridle, and before he could catch the leather strap again, the horse had bolted away into the night.

Still keeping a firm grip on the buckskin's reins, Shannon knelt beside Esteban in the wet sand.

"How badly are you hurt?" he asked.

"My leg was caught under the horse when it fell." Esteban gasped. "I think it is broken."

"Just lie still while I take a look," Shannon said, trying to keep his voice calm. It was easier to make himself heard now that the storm was passing.

It was still too dark to see much, but feeling along Esteban's leg, Shannon encountered the tell-tale bulge where the bone had snapped. Esteban winced in pain as Shannon touched the swelling.

"It's broken, all right," Shannon said. "But don't worry. The storm is letting up, and we'll soon have you out of. . . ."

He paused. From somewhere in the darkness a strange roaring noise could now be heard. As he listened it grew steadily louder—a sound like an express train bearing down on them.

Shannon realized immediately what it was. They were at the bottom of a dry riverbed, and the rain pouring into the river upstream had created one of the dreaded flash floods of which he and Ramón had so recently spoken.

Shannon's mind raced. In minutes, perhaps seconds, the flood would be upon them, and he was standing directly in its path at the bottom of a slope too steep to climb with a crippled man lying at his feet. For a brief moment, he felt like laughing. Over the years so many outlaws and gunmen had tried to kill him and failed, and now a simple rainstorm might do the job for them.

Esteban had also heard the rumble of the approaching flash flood, and he too knew exactly what it was.

*"Dios mio!"* he exclaimed. "We will be drowned!"

He struggled to get up, but the agony of his broken leg sent him back to the ground, crying out in pain.

"Go, Señor Shannon!" he cried. "Leave me! Save yourself while you can!"

"Not likely," Shannon said.

He bent down and grasped Esteban's arm, then pulled him up and heaved him over the shoulders of the startled buckskin. This done, Shannon leapt into the saddle, and then, holding Esteban's belt to prevent him from sliding off the horse's back, kicked the animal into a gallop down the wash, away from the oncoming flood. The clouds had thinned and a little weak moonlight was filtering through providing Shannon with just enough light to give him hope of seeing a way out of the riverbed—if there was one. He urged the buckskin forward, looking intently right and left for some avenue of escape.

"We will never make it!" Esteban cried, clinging to the saddle horn. "The water moves too fast for us to outrun it!"

"Oh, be quiet," Shannon said. "We're not dead yet."

But he knew that Esteban was right. No horse, especially not one carrying double, could outrun the waters of a flash flood. There was one chance and one chance only—that as they raced along the winding riverbed he would somehow, in the dim light, see a way up out of the trap, a break in the cliff, a lessening of the slope where they could climb out of the ravine before they were overwhelmed by the oncoming water.

But no break appeared, and before they had gone a hundred yards the sound behind them had risen to a mighty crescendo. Shannon turned and his stomach tightened as he saw a solid wall of black water come crashing around the bend behind them. The foaming crest was a good eight feet high, and it pounded viciously at the cliffs as it swept inexorably toward Shannon and Esteban. There were uprooted trees in the flood, and even small boulders were being washed along by the irresistible force of the racing water. Horse and men would be crushed and swept away to their deaths in a matter of moments.

And then Shannon saw it—a defile just ahead leading up toward the top of the cliffs. There was no time to guess whether the horse could climb it, or whether the thundering water would wash up the defile as the crest of the flood passed, dragging them back down into the maelstrom. With no other choice, Shannon turned the buckskin toward the slope at full gallop, praying that the defile ran all the way to the top and that the overburdened horse would not trip or fall in the narrow, rocky opening.

Urged on by Shannon's impassioned shouts, the buckskin plunged up the steep slope in great bounds, slipping on the rocks but keeping its feet, laboring valiantly to carry its heavy load to safety. Below them, the flood reached the mouth of the defile, and a wave of water came roiling up the slope behind them. For a moment it swirled around the buckskin's hind legs, cutting away the soil beneath its hooves and trying to suck them all down to a cruel death. Then, in one final, heart-bursting effort, the stallion gained the top of the cliff and with a last prodigious leap came out onto the high, flat ground beyond, safe at last from the lethal floodwaters.

Shannon reined in the spent buckskin and then, as carefully as he could, eased Esteban to the ground.

"Are you all right, *amigo?*" Shannon asked, dismounting beside him. He knew that the trip up the rough defile on the back of a struggling horse must have caused the vaquero great agony from his broken leg, but Esteban had the toughness of his Spanish forebears, and he lay back on the ground, grinning.

"*Santa Maria,*" he said reverently. "That was close, no?"

"Very close," Shannon said. "Without a certain very game horse under us, we'd be dead at the bottom of that riverbed by now."

He walked over to the buckskin. The stallion was standing patiently with its reins dragging, its flanks heaving as it fought to regain its breath after its exertions. Shannon put his arm around the animal's neck and stood there for a long time, resting his head on its shoulder and blessing the providence that had brought this magnificent animal into his life so many years ago.

## Chapter Ten

W hen Esteban had been attended to as well as was possible, Ramón sought out Shannon.

"I'll send a man back with Esteban," he said. "What do we do now, *Patrón?*"

*An excellent question.* Shannon thought. *We've already lost nearly half of our men, the herd's tracks were probably washed out by the storm, and our chances of picking up the trail before daylight are virtually nil. And by then we'll have lost another six or eight hours.*

"Let's keep going," he said finally. "Even if we can't see the tracks, we know they were still traveling southeast, and it's not likely they would change directions now. We'll just keep heading that way and hope for the best."

They rode through the night, occasionally stopping to look for signs of the herd. Once or twice they found indi-

71

cations that cattle had passed, but the rain had made it almost impossible to estimate how long ago that had been.

Shannon grew increasingly restless. If the rustlers had changed course, he was leading his men further off in the wrong direction every hour. At last he conceded to himself that it would be best to stop, let everyone rest, and then move on at daylight, when they might be able to pick up the trail.

He passed the word to the men and was about to dismount when, far off in the distance, a faint glimmer of light caught his eye. He slipped his binoculars out of his saddle-bag and stared through them at the gleam. It did not look like a lamp in a window, as would have been the case if this were someone's ranch house, and besides, there were very few settlers in this region. What was it, then?

"Campfire," he said, handing Ramón the binoculars. Ramón fumbled with the glasses, got them focused, and looked.

"I think you are right," Ramón said. "A fire built near some rocks, so that the light reflects off of them."

"The people we're following would have to be pretty stupid to build a fire knowing we're coming up behind them," Shannon mused. "Still, it's always a great mistake to overestimate your enemy. Let's see if we can get close without them hearing us."

They led their horses cautiously forward over the stony ground, fully aware that an iron shoe striking a rock might instantly alert the people they were stalking. As they came closer to the source of the firelight, Shannon brought them to a halt.

"That's near enough," he said. "We'll leave a man to hold the horses here and go the rest of the way on foot. Walk softly, *muchachos*. We want to get a good look at them before they know we're here."

They had gone only a few more yards when they heard the sound of cattle moving about ahead of them. Warning the vaqueros to wait, Shannon crawled forward through the dry brush and found himself looking down into a shallow depression. The depression was filled with cattle—two hundred head or more, Shannon guessed. It was too dark to see the brands. A hundred yards beyond the depression, a small fire was burning beneath a rocky ledge. Three men were sitting beside it.

Ramón crawled up beside Shannon and regarded the animals gathered below.

"Watch out for the nighthawk," Shannon whispered. "Somebody must be down there minding the cattle."

Ramón touched Shannon's shoulder and pointed to the opposite side of the depression. A horseman was making his way slowly around the edge of the herd.

"Yes, there he is," Shannon murmured. "That's going to complicate things a little."

They moved back a few yards and debated the matter in low tones.

"I need to see those brands," Shannon said. "Odds are they're ours, but I want to be sure before we jump those people sitting by the fire."

"We will have to silence the guard, then," Ramón said. He slid his knife out of its sheath. "I will arrange it."

"Don't kill him," Shannon said. "These people could be innocent cowhands who just happened to get in our way. Until I see the brand on those animals, I don't want to hurt anybody unnecessarily."

Ramón nodded.

"I will keep the man quiet while you look at the brands," he said. "Shall we go now?"

They crawled back to the edge of the depression and Shannon waited breathlessly as Ramón moved away down the slope and disappeared into the night. It would be a delicate task to silence the man watching the herd without harming him, and Shannon hoped that Ramón would not forget that the identity of the herders was as yet unknown. If the cattle proved to be from Rancho Alvarez, that of course would be a different matter.

Below him he heard a low grunt and then something hit the ground with a thump. The nearest cattle stirred and looked curiously around, then lost interest. In a few moments Ramón gave a low whistle, and Shannon descended into the darkness after him.

The herder was stretched out on his stomach on the ground. Ramón was sitting on top of him, holding the point of his knife against the man's throat. The herder's now-riderless horse stood nearby, its reins dragging. Ramón had stuffed a bandana into the herder's mouth, but the man was still managing to utter a string of muffled curses through the sweaty rag. Most of the oaths alluded to the marital state of Ramón's parents and his relationship to a variety of animals. Shannon knelt down beside the man.

"Mister," Shannon said, "if I were you I wouldn't say anything else about Señor Peralta's mother. He's a little sensitive on the subject, and that knife he's got against your throat is very, very sharp. So it would be in your best interest to just lie there and keep your mouth shut. Understand?"

The man grunted another malediction, but stopped struggling and lay still. Shannon got up and moved silently toward the nearest steers, stepping carefully to avoid alarming them. Range cattle were often bad tempered and hostile, and when so inclined were perfectly capable of goring or trampling a man on foot who came too near. These beasts merely regarded Shannon with bovine indifference as he approached. *Perhaps they're tired,* Shannon thought. *They've been pushed pretty hard the last couple of days, and they may just be too worn out to be ornery.*

The bottom of the depression was hidden from the view of the men at the campfire on the ledge, and so Shannon crouched down and daringly lit a match, hoping the small sound and the sudden spark of light would not cause the cattle to stampede. Again, the animals merely looked at him. Moving a few steps closer, he held the match up high enough to give him light to read the brands on their flanks. The match flared and dwindled. Shannon caught his breath and quickly extinguished the dying flame. The brand on the flanks of the cattle was that of Rancho Alvarez. They had found at least a portion of their lost herd.

But why only four men and a few animals? Why had they been separated from the main herd? He crept back to the place where Ramón and his prisoner waited.

"They're ours," he said to Ramón.

*"Bueno,"* Ramón said. "Now I kill this *puerco,* yes?"

The outlaw on the ground cursed again and tried to get up.

Shannon shoved him back to the earth and bent over him.

"Last warning, mister," he growled. "One more sound out of you—just one more squeak—and I'll tell my friend with the knife to cut you into little pieces. You understand me?"

The man glared ferociously at him, but lay still.

They lifted him to his feet, and Ramón prodded him up the hill at knifepoint with Shannon close behind. Creeping through the brush, they moved back to the spot where they had left the other vaqueros. Briefly, Shannon explained the situation to them while Ramón trussed their captive up and gagged him properly.

"We're going into the camp," Shannon said. "There's still a little breeze, and that will cover some of the sound of our approach. Keep your rifles ready—there are only three of them, but these are the men who murdered your *compadres* and shot the Señora. They're desperate and dangerous—remember that. If possible, I want to take them alive, because I want to question them, but if they try to shoot it out, take no chances—kill them immediately. Is that clear?"

The men nodded and silently readied their weapons. Ramón told Pablo to hold the horses and stand guard over the tied-up outlaw.

"Keep a sharp eye on him, Pablo," Shannon said. "He's a tough customer, or thinks he is, and he'll jump you if he gets the chance."

"I will watch him carefully, Señor," Pablo said. "You can count on me. Remember, my cousin was among those they killed."

"All right, Pablo," Shannon said. "I'm relying on you. Now, everybody ready?"

Moving with infinite care, Shannon led the rest of the vaqueros around the top of the depression, signaling them to spread out so that they would not be approaching the campfire all bunched together.

Within moments they were only a few feet from the ledge, almost at the edge of the circle of light cast by the fire. Shannon saw that the shelf where the rustlers were sitting was actually the mouth of a large cave that extended back into the rocky hillside. He studied the entrance carefully, but the interior was pitch black, and he could not determine how far back it went or whether anyone was inside.

The men around the fire gave no sign of having heard their approach, and Shannon wondered at their lack of vigilance. Then he saw the whiskey bottle being passed around among them, and understood. Thinking for some reason that they were safe from pursuit, the outlaws had not only built a fire but had also proceeded to get drunk. Well, they would soon regret their mistake.

He motioned to the vaqueros to take cover, then moved behind a rocky outcropping. When he saw that the vaqueros were in position, he slipped the Colt silently out of its holster and prepared to step out into the open.

At that moment a loud scream echoed out of the darkness behind them. The whiskey bottle splintered on the rocks as the three rustlers jumped up and whirled around, drawing their revolvers. Their eyes were wide as they stared out into the darkness, trying to locate the source of the terrible shriek.

"Was that Lefty who yelled?" one of them said.

"Naw," said another, "but it came from that direction. Let's get over there and take a look."

Cursing the turn of events that had alerted the rustlers and robbed him of the element of surprise, Shannon leapt out into the circle of firelight, his Colt at the ready.

"Reach!" he said. "You've got a half-dozen rifles pointed at your bellies! The first man who tries anything is dead meat!"

Realizing that they were perfect targets in the firelight, the startled outlaws froze, staring goggle-eyed at Shannon.

"Who are you, mister?" one of them asked. "What do you want?"

"I'm a United States marshal," Shannon replied, "and you're all under arrest for cattle theft and murder. I'm taking you back to Los Santos to stand trial. Now holster those six-guns, then unbuckle your gunbelts and put them on the ground. And do it nice and easy, if you want to live to see the sunrise."

"Don't do it, boys!" one of the rustlers warned. "If they take us they'll hang us sure!"

His companions hesitated, weighing their chances.

"You're right," Shannon said. "You *will* hang when we get you back to Los Santos. Or you can die right here, right now. Your choice."

He knew that he should not have said it, for otherwise the men might have surrendered. But the anger burning in Shannon's heart had made him indifferent to the rustlers' fate, and, as he admitted to himself later, he had deliberately goaded them, half-hoping they would resist.

They wavered for a split second, then made their decision. Raising their pistols, they fired point-blank at Shannon. Fortunately for him, surprise and fear had made their hands unsteady, and the three slugs whirred harmlessly past him. Without waiting for a second shot, the outlaws turned and fled headlong toward the shelter of the cave entrance.

"Stop them!" Shannon ordered. The vaqueros opened fire, and one of the rustlers went down far short of the cave's mouth. A second volley sent another of the men tumbling into a heap right in the entrance. The third man, however, somehow untouched by the hail of gunfire, made it to the safety of the cave and disappeared.

The vaqueros began firing blindly into the opening. The crash of the rifles echoed back at them from the depths of the cavern, and Shannon could hear the bullets ricocheting off the walls like angry bees.

Shannon grunted in disgust. They could no longer see

the fugitive, and there was little chance of anyone hitting him with a stray bullet if he was well back from the entrance.

"Hold your fire, men," he shouted to the vaqueros. The shooting stopped.

Shannon walked further forward into the firelight.

"You in the cave," he called. "Can you hear me?"

His answer was a stream of filthy oaths reverberating out of the cavern.

"Drop the gun and come on out," Shannon said loudly. "You can't get away—we've got the entrance covered."

"If you want me so much, come in and get me!" the unseen man yelled. "I ain't gonna walk out there and let you string me up, you. . . ." Another string of obscenities followed.

"Señor!" called one of the vaqueros. "Someone is coming up the slope behind us."

They shrank back into the rocks, training their rifles toward the sound of this new threat. A moment later Pablo staggered into the firelight. He was clutching his stomach, and his clothes were dark with blood.

"Help me, *amigos,*" Pablo said. Then he stumbled and fell to the ground, moaning.

Shannon and Ramón were immediately beside him. Ramón eased Pablo's hands away from his wound so that he could examine it.

"What happened, Pablo?" Shannon asked.

"He tricked me, Señor," Pablo said. "He began moaning and rolling around on the ground. I took the gag off to find out what was wrong. He said that he was ill and begged me to untie his hands. I did not know what to do, Señor. I did not want him to die. But when I cut the rope that was around his wrists, he pulled a knife out of his boot and stabbed me in the belly. I am sorry, Señor. You set me to guard him, and I failed."

"Easy, Pablo," Shannon said. "What happened to the man? Did he get away?"

"*Sí*, Señor," Pablo whispered. "I could not stop him. He took my horse and rode off. Please forgive me."

"I forgive you, Pablo," Shannon said gently. "Lie quietly now, while we tend to your wound."

Shannon looked at Ramón, who had opened Pablo's shirt to examine the injury. Ramón shook his head slightly, then looked away. For a moment Shannon thought that he saw tears in the old vaquero's eyes.

Shannon rested his hand briefly on Pablo's shoulder, the sorrow rising in him. Pablo was a favorite among the vaqueros, a childlike man of little intellect but infinite kindness. Charlotte was particularly fond of him, for he had been her companion and guardian since she was a child. And now he lay dying, the victim of his own goodness and an outlaw's brutal cunning. Shannon found himself wondering how many more of the men of Rancho Alvarez would have to die before the rest would be left alone to live out their lives in peace.

Shannon stood up and stared angrily at the mouth of the cave. There was no time for grief now. That would have to come later. Meanwhile, he still had one more outlaw to deal with.

"Any sign of him?" he asked the vaqueros who were watching the entrance.

"No, Señor," one of them replied. "He has not come out. We can hear him moving around in there, but we cannot see him. The cave is deep, I think."

"What shall we do, Señor?" Ramón asked, rising to stand at Shannon's side. "Shall we wait for him? Sooner or later he will become hungry and thirsty, and then he will come out."

"Maybe," Shannon said. "Maybe not. He knows he's a dead man either way, and he sounds like a real hard case. He might just decide to end it here and take a few of us with him."

"Then what are your orders, *Patrón?*"

Shannon was thinking rapidly. Even if the man eventually came out voluntarily, they could not afford to wait that long. Whatever the reason for the presence of these men and the small herd here, the remainder of the gang and the vast majority of the cattle were moving further away from them every moment. Therefore, there was only one solution.

"Wait here," he said to Ramón. "Keep the entrance covered until I come out. If anyone walks out of there and it isn't me, shoot him."

"You are going in after him?" Ramón said in disbelief. "It is madness, *Patrón!*"

"It's a necessity," Shannon said. "I don't like it any more than you do, but there's no other way."

He reloaded the Colt, then walked over to the campfire and kicked it apart. The flames died and the ledge was thrown into darkness. Now, at least, he would not be silhouetted against the firelight when he went in. He paused, glancing up at the sky. The clouds were gone now and the moon had reappeared. It was a full moon, bright and beautiful against the deep blue backdrop of the night. Shannon briefly found himself wondering if he would ever see it again. Then he cast the thought from his mind. He had a job to do, and pessimism would not help. Either he would survive the next few minutes or he would not; there was no use being morbid about it.

He waved at Ramón and then, Colt in hand and moving as silently as possible, he walked into the cavern.

## Chapter Eleven

Even with the reappearance of the moon, the night outside the cave was dark. Inside the cave, the blackness was absolute. As soon as he was safely through the entrance, Shannon pressed his back against the rough wall and then slid forward, holding the cocked Colt in his right hand and feeling for obstructions with his left. His pulse was racing, and in the confined space of the cavern the sound of his breathing seemed magnified a hundred times.

*He must know I'm coming,* Shannon thought. *He's bound to hear me, unless he's stone deaf.*

The footing was uneven, and rocks of all sizes littered the floor of the cave. Shannon slid his feet forward very carefully, trying to avoid kicking anything. Suddenly, his heart jumped violently as his groping left hand encountered something round and smooth and damp, right next to him

84

at eye level. He had almost squeezed the trigger of his six-gun before he realized that it was merely an outcropping in the rocky wall and not a human head.

But the gasp that had escaped him as he touched it must have signaled his position, for without warning the cave exploded in flame and noise, and from directly ahead a bullet screamed past Shannon, ricocheting wildly off the walls before it spent itself somewhere in the darkness.

Shannon gulped. Even in the pitch black the outlaw's bullet had nearly found him. *The good news is, he missed me,* Shannon told himself. *The bad news is, he didn't miss me by very much. He must have ears like a wolf's to zero in on me like that, just because of a few small sounds. This is going to be tricky.*

By firing first however, the outlaw had given Shannon an advantage. The muzzle flash had impressed an indelible image of the cave's topography on Shannon's brain. He now knew that on the left side of the cave were huge boulders, while on the right the wall and floor were relatively flat and open. He crouched low and moved quickly across the passage. He was trying to anticipate its width accurately in order to avoid a collision with the rocks on the other side, but his calculation was a little off, and he bumped heavily into the opposite wall. The barrel of his six-gun scraped along the limestone, and immediately another shot boomed out, again illuminating the cavern like a lightning flash and shaking the walls with its explosion. Dust and small rocks showered down on Shannon as the echoes of the shot died away.

Working from the image left in his mind by the second gun flash, Shannon dropped to his knees and began to crawl forward. In the brief light of the muzzle blast, he had been able to estimate his opponent's position very closely. The outlaw was crouched down behind a rock ledge, a horizontal ridge perhaps three feet high that ran across the floor of the cave some twenty feet ahead of him.

Now the game was truly getting dangerous. Shannon was a man of steady nerves—he would not have survived long in his profession if he had been otherwise—but the tension generated by the deadly game of blindman's bluff he was playing was taking its toll on him. Had the gunman seen him in the light of the last muzzle flash? Quite possibly, which meant that even now he could be drawing a bead on Shannon's position, waiting for the one final tiny sound that would bring a bullet smashing into Shannon's body.

There was a scuffling somewhere ahead of him, and Shannon knew that his antagonist was changing his location, trying to deceive Shannon as to his whereabouts. The noise moved several yards to the right and seemed to recede back into the cavern a little. *Keep backing up, pal,* Shannon thought. *This hole can't run back into the cliff forever, and when you get to the end of it, you're mine.*

He began to crawl forward again, trying not to let anything metal—belt buckle, badge, or six-gun—strike rock. But again the outlaw fired, and this time the slug passed close enough to Shannon's face to send a splinter of rock stinging across his cheek. He could feel a trickle of blood running down his jaw, but he knew it was just a minor wound, and, in any case, there was no time to worry about it. The vibration of the gunshot had loosened more material from the ceiling, and several large pieces struck Shannon's head and shoulders as they fell. *Looks like I'll have a few bruises to show for this little adventure,* he thought to himself. *Well, scratches and bruises are better than bullet holes. Let's just hope I don't pick up any of those. That gunslinger must have been born in the dark, the way he shoots in it.*

Again Shannon quietly shifted position, hoping to throw off his antagonist's aim. As he moved, his hand encountered a bulge in the rock just ahead of him, a protrusion from the wall that would be enough to shield him from the gunman's fire for a moment.

"Give it up, mister!" Shannon said loudly, crouching behind the rock. "There's no way out of here for you. Even if you get me, the rest are waiting outside for you. You'll be cut down before you get three feet from the mouth of the cave."

"Maybe," the bandit yelled, "but you won't know the difference, because I'm gonna gun you down and leave you in this hole to rot. You're in your coffin right now."

The gunman fired again, and this time a heavy rumble preceded the crash of several slabs of rock falling further back in the cave. It dawned on Shannon that further gunfire might well bring down still larger rocks from the ceiling or even cause a complete collapse, burying both the hunter and the hunted.

"Don't be a fool," Shannon said. "Can't you see that the

gunshots are going to knock this whole place down right on your head?"

"Your head's in here too, lawman," the outlaw said. "Now cut the palaver and come and get me. I'm just waiting to put a bullet in your gut."

Shannon crouched lower behind the outcropping and considered the situation. It was clear the man wasn't going to surrender. Furthermore, time was passing, and time was not on Shannon's side. The man who had knifed Pablo and escaped must even now be riding hard to warn his comrades that retribution was close behind them. Armed with that knowledge, they might scatter the herd and then scatter themselves, putting both men and cattle beyond Shannon's reach. He had to resolve the present impasse somehow.

He began to slide his body forward across the uneven floor toward the gunman's last known position. If he could just get close enough. . . .

The man fired again. The bullet went far above Shannon's lowered head, but the flash was close and in its light Shannon could see that the outlaw was straight ahead of him, not thirty feet away and crouched behind another rocky ridge running across the cave floor.

Shannon took a deep breath. The next few moments would tell the tale. Charlotte might well be a widow in thirty seconds.

Clenching his teeth, he leaped up and charged at the gunman, firing rapidly as he came. The noise was deafening, and now whole portions of the cavern's ceiling began to fall around him, but he did not stop. The rapid gunflashes clearly revealed his enemy's location, and Shannon reached the ledge in a few great strides. The rustler had leapt up from his place of concealment and was firing blindly back at Shannon now. Shannon could feel the wind of the bullets passing, but none struck him, and then he was hurdling onto the rock ledge, poised above the frantic gunman. The outlaw fired one last desperate shot, and it provided the final glimpse of him that Shannon needed. He pulled the trigger of the Colt one more time, and in its muzzle flash he saw the man lurching backward against the cavern wall, screaming and clutching at his chest with his left hand as he raised his six-gun to fire point-blank into Shannon's face.

Then Shannon was upon him, driving his shoulder into the injured man, slamming him back against the wall of the cave with tremendous force. The man screamed a second time as Shannon pinned him to the wall, groping blindly to catch the gunman's wrist before he could fire again. In the darkness Shannon's hand closed instead over the barrel of the six-gun. He could feel the cylinder turning against his palm as the outlaw struggled to cock the weapon. Shannon ripped the gun out of the man's hand by the barrel and smashed the butt across his opponent's unseen face. Again the man shrieked, and this time he went down in a heap at Shannon's feet and lay there, moaning.

Shannon extracted a match from his pocket and scratched it against the rock wall. The sudden flare of the match was almost blinding to eyes that had been in total darkness for so long, but by its brief, flickering light Shannon saw that his adversary was twisted up against the wall of the cavern, his hands clutching convulsively at his bloody shirt as he whimpered in pain.

There was no time for Shannon to savor his victory. The cavern was now filled with a constant rumbling, and more and more debris tumbled down around them. A huge slab of rock broke loose somewhere directly above them and came crashing down. One of the fragments struck Shannon a glancing blow that half stunned him. On his hands and knees, the match now extinguished, Shannon grasped the gunman's legs and began to drag him over the fallen rock toward the cave entrance—or at least where he fancied the cave entrance to be. He knew that in the total darkness he might have become disoriented, and could well be going the wrong way, farther back into the cave. More rock came down, and it occurred to Shannon suddenly that so much had fallen that it could be blocking the entrance completely, entombing him with the wounded outlaw forever. The prediction of the gunman that Shannon was already in his coffin might well prove true.

"Ramón!" Shannon shouted. "Show a light!"

Immediately a burst of flame pierced the gloom, and then another and another. Shannon saw with infinite relief that Ramón and several vaqueros were climbing over the fallen rocks toward him, carrying crude torches made from pieces of tied-together brushwood.

"Señor Shannon!" Ramón called. "Where are you?"

"Here," Shannon replied. "Back here. Be careful—more of the ceiling could break loose at any moment."

As they approached him through the debris, Shannon sat down on the rock ledge and tried valiantly to slow his rapid breathing. At last they reached him, and relief flooded through him as strong hands helped him off the ledge and led him, bruised and battered but gratefully alive, back toward the mouth of the cave and out into the beautiful, blessed moonlight.

The wounded outlaw was treated less tenderly. The vaqueros dragged him out by the feet, ignoring his cries as his head struck repeatedly against the rocks now littering the cavern floor. When they had him outside, they dumped him unceremoniously on the stony ground and stood by expectantly, waiting for Shannon.

"Get that fire going again," Shannon said, wiping the rock dust out of his eyes. "I want to get a look at this thug."

He turned to Ramón.

"How is Pablo?" he said, dreading the answer.

"He is dead, Señor," Ramón said sadly. "And the *bandito* who murdered him has gotten away—I sent men after him while you were in the cave, but they could not find him in the dark."

He gestured at the man they had dragged out of the cavern.

"But at least we have this one, thanks to you. We will kill him a little bit at a time, I think."

The fire had been rekindled now, and Shannon walked over to the wounded gunman who lay stretched out on the ground. His breathing was labored, and it was obvious that the last bullet Shannon had fired had pierced both his lungs.

"Time to talk, tough guy," Shannon said, leaning down. "Where have your friends gone with the rest of the herd?"

The gunman spat at him.

"I ain't tellin' you nothin'," he snarled.

Shannon drew his Colt, flipped open the loading gate, and one by one ejected the empty shell casings and the remaining unfired cartridges from the cylinder. Then, as the wounded gunman watched defiantly, Shannon ostentatiously slipped one round back into the cylinder and spun it rapidly around several times.

The outlaw's mouth was open as he struggled to breathe. Shannon cocked the hammer of the Colt, then leaned down and shoved the barrel of the weapon between the man's teeth.

"Now," Shannon said, "let's try it again, shall we? Where have your fellow felons gone with the herd?"

"I don't know nothin'," the man mumbled sullenly.

Shannon pulled the trigger. The hammer fell harmlessly on an empty chamber. Without removing the gun barrel from the outlaw's mouth, Shannon cocked the hammer again.

"Where?" he said.

"I tell you I dunno," said the outlaw, coughing. His tone was less defiant now, and his eyes were wide with fear.

Shannon pulled the trigger again, and again the hammer fell on an empty chamber. The outlaw flinched; his eyes were now fairly popping out of his head.

"You're crazy!" he howled. "You're gonna blow my head off if you keep doin' that!"

"That's right," Shannon said. "That's exactly what's going to happen if you don't answer my questions. Talk and I'll let you live. Otherwise, you die right now with your brains scattered all over these rocks."

He pulled the trigger again, and once more the click of a hammer falling on an empty chamber echoed along the ledge.

"That's three," Shannon said. "Want to try for four?"

"Stop it!" the outlaw squealed. "If I talk, you promise I'll live?"

"I said so, didn't I?" Shannon said. He cocked the hammer again, very slowly.

"All right, all right!" the outlaw said. His breath was coming in ragged gasps now, and his voice was growing weaker. "Don't shoot. I'll talk. Whaddaya wanna know?"

"That's better," Shannon said, removing the gun muzzle from the man's mouth. "Now, one more time—where are your friends taking the herd?"

"Texas," the man said. "They're goin' across the border into Texas."

"I had a brief chat with one of your *compadres* back in Casa Cochina," Shannon said. "He mentioned something about selling the cattle to the '*gringo* army.' What did he mean?

"It's Snyder," the outlaw said. "He knows somebody at Fort Lister who'll buy 'em, no questions asked. They're takin' the rest of the herd there."

"Snyder's the boss of your gang?"

"Yeah, blast his hide. I never liked him—nobody likes

him—but he's got that connection at the fort, so we let him call the shots. You know him? Snyder, I mean?"

"I know him," Shannon said bitterly.

An evil smile twisted the outlaw's face.

"You're Shannon, ain'tcha?" he said. "Snyder told us all about your ranch and your herd—said it would be the biggest cattle job anybody ever pulled."

"Who killed our vaqueros on the night the cattle were taken?"

"I dunno who brought 'em down right off. We was all shootin'. Most of your cowhands was only wounded at first, but later Snyder came back and shot them all dead, right where they lay. He said he had a score to settle with—what's your spread's name—'Rancho Alvarez.' Yeah, he had some kinda grudge against you, all right. He enjoyed pluggin' your people too. He said it was like shootin' fish in a barrel."

"And none of the rest of you tried to stop him from killing wounded men while they lay helpless on the ground?"

The outlaw looked puzzled.

"Why should we?" he said. "They was just Mexicans, wasn't they?"

Shannon clenched his fists, fighting back the urge to smash the man's face in. He might have done it, but at that moment the rustler was seized with a long spasm of coughing, and Shannon forced himself to wait patiently until it ended.

Finally the bandit regained his breath and lay back weakly on the earth.

"My chest hurts somethin' awful," he whimpered.

"No doubt," Shannon said.

"Ain't I said enough yet?" the man whined. "I gotta rest now. I ain't feelin' so good."

"One more question," Shannon said. "What were the four of you doing here with just a few head? Were you left behind to bushwhack us?"

"Hunh? Naw, nothin' like that," the man replied. His voice was barely a whisper now. "We split off about five miles back," he went on. "We figured you'd follow the main herd—didn't think you'd bother to come after us. That bunch of longhorns down in the draw there is our share of the pickin's. We was takin' 'em back to our spread in west Texas. We was gonna change the brands and sell them to one of the cattle buyers at the railroad later. They pay better than Snyder's man at the fort."

Another coughing spell shook him. It went on for a long time, and after it was over he fell back, exhausted.

Ramón had been standing nearby, watching the proceedings with great interest. Now he looked with contempt at the wounded outlaw.

"What shall we do with him, *Patrón?*" he asked.

"No need to do anything with him," Shannon said. "He's dying."

"Dyin'?" the rustler cried, struggling to sit up. "You said I'd live! You promised that if I told you what you wanted to know, I'd live!"

Shannon reached out with the toe of his boot and shoved the doomed man back to the ground—hard.

"I lied," Shannon said, and walked away.

## Chapter Twelve

The dawn was breaking as they climbed into their saddles once more. Two vaqueros had been detailed to take the recovered cattle back to Rancho Alvarez. It would be a long ride and a difficult task for only two men, but Shannon knew that they could spare no more. Men dead, men wounded who had to be escorted back, men left behind at Casa Cochina—each incident had taken its toll. Now two more had to be sent back, and only Shannon, Ramón, and five others were left to resume the pursuit of the main herd.

"It is not enough, *Patrón,*" Ramón said. "When we find the herd, we will have to take it many miles back to the *rancho*. Even if we lose no more men, it will be a difficult task for the few of us who are left to drive nearly two thousand head so far. We will lose many animals on the way."

"We may not have two thousand head to drive by the time we find them," Shannon said regretfully. "Besides, we can take them to Casa Cochina first. We left men there to guard the señora, and also wounded men who should be well enough by then to help us."

Thanks to the dying outlaw's information, they now knew that, as Shannon had feared, blinded by the thunderstorm, they had missed the track of the main herd, never noticing that it had turned east directly toward the Texas border. It had been mere chance that the smaller group of men and cattle had separated from the main body just before the storm, and pure coincidence that Shannon's decision to continue southeast—a bad decision, Shannon thought, blaming himself—had caused them to pass within sight of the telltale campfire. However, he decided ruefully, a bad decision had combined with good luck to enable them to regain at least a small portion of that which had been stolen from them.

But now they had to ride even harder to make up the time they had lost at the cave, and so they hurried off toward the northeast, a direction that Shannon and Ramón agreed ought to enable them to cut the trail of the eastbound main herd without backtracking completely.

They had been riding less than an hour when Ramón reined up abruptly and pointed at something on the ground.

"Look, *Patrón*," he said. "The hoofmarks of a single horse, traveling in nearly the same direction as we are."

"Yes," said Shannon, examining the marks. "One horse

only, going a little north of east. Anybody recognize the prints?"

The vaqueros came forward and looked.

"I know them, *Señor*," said one of them. "It is Pablo's horse. I have seen those tracks many times back at the *rancho*."

"Well," Shannon said, "if it's Pablo's horse, the man who killed him must be riding it. He's probably trying to catch up with the rest of the gang, just as we are. Let's see if we can catch up to him first. If he reaches them before we do, he'll give them warning that we're coming."

Ramón was still examining the hoofprints.

"We should not have much difficulty catching him, Señor," he said. "The horse is lame, and goes slowly. Look."

Shannon reexamined the prints, and saw at once that Ramón was right. The horse was limping noticeably.

"That animal isn't going to get far carrying a rider," Shannon said. "Come on."

He spurred the buckskin into a gallop and started after the escaping killer. The others whipped up their horses as well, but the buckskin was the best of their mounts, and soon began to draw well ahead of the vaqueros. A mile melted away under the stallion's flashing hooves, and then another. Shannon was just about to slow the pace for the horse's sake when he saw in the distance ahead a dark shape moving slowly across the land. Shannon urged the buckskin onward, and within a few moments had drawn near enough to the unknown rider to see that the horse upon which the man was sitting was limping badly.

*Why doesn't that scum turn the horse loose and walk?* Shannon thought to himself. *He'll cripple the animal trying to ride him in that condition.*

Because he loved horses and would never have mistreated one in such a manner, it did not immediately occur to Shannon that a man who would murder other men in cold blood would hardly hesitate to abuse a horse, especially if it might ensure his escape.

Shannon was rapidly closing the gap between himself and the fleeing outlaw. *He'll see me any minute now,* Shannon thought, *and then he'll try to make that poor beast run. Well, it won't be for long.*

At that moment the man, hearing hoofbeats behind him, twisted around in the saddle and looked back at Shannon. His mouth fell open and he bent low over the tired horse's neck, whipping it in an effort to get it to go faster. But the animal could not respond, and after a short distance it went down, throwing the man to the ground. The outlaw rolled over, leapt up, and began to run, trying to reach a small ravine just ahead in which he could hide from his pursuer. Shannon saw at once that the man had enough of a head start to make it to cover before Shannon could reach him.

*No more standoffs in the rocks,* Shannon thought to himself. *No more dead vaqueros or time wasted in unnecessary gun battles.* He brought the buckskin to a halt beside Pablo's fallen animal and slipped his Winchester out of the saddle scabbard. He levered a cartridge into the chamber and then took careful aim at the center of the fleeing man's back. The Winchester bucked and the man went down, skidding forward on his face in the dust. Shannon shoved the rifle back into its scabbard and rode over to the still figure on the ground. Ramón and the others came riding up and reined in beside him.

"Dead, I think," Ramón said calmly, looking at the body. "An excellent shot, Señor."

"I never used to shoot people in the back," Shannon said sadly. "But then, I've been doing a lot of things lately that I've never done before."

Ramón shrugged.

"It was necessary," he said. "That is enough."

"Necessity is the author of many cruelties," Shannon replied, quoting a half-forgotten line he had read in a book long ago.

A shadow passed over the little group as they stood looking at the dead man. Shannon glanced up. One of the Southwest's ubiquitous vultures had detected death, and was preparing to take advantage of it. Within moments, two more of the great birds joined the circle in the sky.

Shannon looked back at Pablo's horse, lying a few yards away up the trail. "Some of you get that animal on its feet," he said. "If it's not badly lamed, we'll take it along with us. We couldn't save Pablo, but perhaps we can save his horse."

The feathered shadows passed overhead again.

"What about the *bandito?*" Ramón asked, watching the circling vultures. "Shall we bury him?"

"No," Shannon said curtly.

"But we cannot just let him lie there," Ramón protested, looking again at the vultures overhead. "He was a bad man and deserved to die, but he still has a right to a decent burial." A few moments ago the old vaquero would cheerfully have cut the man's throat, but now the thought of leaving his corpse to be devoured by birds of prey was repugnant to him.

Shannon thought of Pablo and Pablo's lamed horse and Charlotte and all the other friends they had left behind them, injured or dying because of this dead man and his accomplices.

"Leave him," Shannon said. "Buzzards have rights too."

## Chapter Thirteen

T he weather was hotter now, and the sun beat down upon the riders of Rancho Alvarez as they moved eastward.

"We should be in Texas soon," Shannon said, shading his eyes with his hand and studying the terrain ahead. "In fact, we may have crossed the Texas border already."

"Look, *Patrón,*" Ramón said. "Cattle tracks ahead. We have found their trail again."

"Excellent," said Shannon. "Now all we have to do is find the herd itself."

They began to follow the tracks eastward. As they rode, Ramón removed his hat and wiped the band to clear it of some of the perspiration that was staining it.

"This 'Fort Lister,' " he said. "How far is it from the border?"

"A couple of hours, I'd say," Shannon said. "I know it only from the maps. I've never been there."

"I do not like this, *Patrón*," Ramón said unhappily. "The Yankee army has not been kind to our people in this part of the country, and I would much prefer not to go among them now."

"They're usually not too fond of federal marshals either," Shannon replied, "but if Snyder took the cattle there, we have no choice but to follow."

"I will kill this Snyder fellow twice, I think," Ramón muttered.

Shannon held up his hand for them to bring their horses to a halt.

"Up there," Shannon said, gesturing. "On that little rise to the south of us. We've got company."

Nine horsemen sat astride their mounts atop a small ridge a short distance ahead of them, observing their approach intently. The horsemen made no move to flee or attack, but just waited there, silently watching as Shannon and the others drew near.

"Shall we open fire?" Ramón asked Shannon, starting to reach for his rifle.

"Not yet," Shannon said. "Let's find out who they are, first. They don't act like cattle rustlers on the run."

They were now close enough for Shannon to see them more clearly. The men were lean, sunburned, and hard looking. They sat atop their horses with an ease that spoke of long hours in the saddle, and their eyes were keen and steady. Repeating rifles adorned their saddles, and most of them were wearing two six-guns. A few had belts of ammunition slung across their chests.

*"Cuidado, compadres,"* Shannon said quietly as they drew nearer to the waiting riders. "Be careful. Whoever these men are, they're well armed and they look as if they can take care of themselves. No one is to touch a weapon unless I do. Understood?"

The vaqueros murmured agreement. Shannon kicked the buckskin and rode up to the tall, gaunt man who was waiting a few steps in advance of the rest of the unknown party, leaning on his saddle horn. All of the strangers appeared calm and relaxed, but Shannon knew enough about men and about danger to see that these people were on high alert, ready to draw their weapons and open fire in an instant if necessary.

*They can't be the rustlers,* Shannon thought, as he reined up a few feet from the leader. *But who are they?*

Then he saw the badge on the tall man's shirt. It was the famous circled star of the Texas Rangers.

"Howdy," said the tall man. "You folks just come over from the New Mexico Territory?

"Yes," Shannon said. "I'm a U.S. Marshal out of Los Santos. Shannon's the name, and these are my vaqueros. You?"

"I'm Captain John Hart, Texas Rangers," the man said. "What brings you this far east, Marshal?"

Shannon explained to him the object of their journey.

"Fort Lister, eh?" Captain Hart said, rubbing his chin. "Somebody's taken some cattle there recently, all right. The tracks you're following lead in that direction. Only seven of you?"

"Only seven of us left," Shannon said. "We've had a couple of arguments with the rustlers along the way. Have you passed through Fort Lister recently?"

Hart shook his head.

"Sorry, no. We're out of Amarillo, trying to catch up to about two hundred Comanche warriors that have jumped the reservation south of here. They got tired of being starved by dishonest Indian agents and decided to express their resentment by burning ranch houses and killing settlers."

"I thought that was the army's business," Shannon said. "Protecting the settlers, I mean, and bringing back Indians who've left the reservation. Aren't they out looking for the Comanches?"

Hart's laugh was harsh.

"Not this part of the army," he said. "Colonel Clinton and his mob prefer to stay nice and snug in their little fort. The only time they come out is to visit the dives outside the gates, slopping up the booze and fighting each other over the saloon girls."

"Hard luck for you," Shannon said. "One company of rangers against a couple of hundred Comanches."

Hart laughed again.

"That's no problem," he said. "With nine Texas Rangers on the job, who needs the army? That bunch of hungover bluebellies would just get in the way. We're the ones those poor Comanches had better worry about."

Shannon grinned. He was familiar with the bravado of the Texas Rangers and their dislike of the army. Both the bravado and the dislike were well founded. The antagonism toward the army dated from the post–Civil War period, when northern troops and carbetbagging politicians bent on punishing the people of Texas for their allegiance to the Confederacy had made mockery of the word "justice" in the Lone Star state. As for the bravado, the Rangers had every right to take pride in their accomplishments, for they had a long record of doing exactly what they said they would do, and doing it with as few men as possible.

"Well, Shannon," Captain Hart said, "I wish you luck at Fort Lister. If we get the Comanches calmed down in time, I'll come back up this way and see if we can give you a hand. But right now I've got some riding to do. We have to get on the trail of those Indians before they scalp too many more Texicans."

He signaled to his men to move out.

"*Adios,* Marshal," he said to Shannon, and then, turning to the vaqueros, he waved and called out *"Buena suerte, muchachos. Vayan con Dios!"*

"Good luck, indeed," said Ramón grumpily when they had gone. "Why do they not ride with us after the rustlers?"

Shannon instinctively came to the defense of his fellow lawmen.

"Ramón," he said, "have you ever seen a frontier ranch house that's been burned to ashes by a Comanche raiding party? Innocent people lying dead on the ground, their scalps missing? Dozens of cattle that have been slaughtered

for no reason? Those Rangers have work to do elsewhere—
urgent work. Now, let's attend to our own business. I want
to reach the fort by dark."

He pulled the buckskin's head around and started once
more along the trail of the stolen herd.

It was midafternoon when they finally caught sight of
Fort Lister. The terrain was flatter here than it had been
during the past days, and the fort was visible long before
they reached it. To their dismay, however, the cattle tracks
they had been following were now becoming very faint.
The wind and the rain had taken their toll upon the hoof-
marks of the Alvarez herd, and soon they were obscured
entirely by hundreds of other tracks, prints new and old left
by cattle and horses, wagons, and other vehicles, all con-
verging upon the fort. An army post in the center of any
underpopulated region was a natural magnet for men and
beasts, and a generation of hoofprints and wheelmarks had
swallowed up all traces of the stolen cattle.

"It appears that they took at least some our cattle to the
fort," Ramón said, "but I cannot be sure. We have lost the
trail, Señor Shannon."

"No matter," Shannon said. "We know they were headed
for the fort. If the herd isn't there, no doubt the army will
be able to tell us where the rustlers have taken it."

"Perhaps," said Ramón gloomily. "You are assuming
that the soldiers will help us, *Patrón*. I am not so certain
of their goodwill."

Shannon ignored this and busied himself with studying

the appearance of the fort as they drew near. It was a large post, with many buildings of various sizes and a stockade fence surrounding some of them—some, but not all. Grouped around the walls of the fort, sometimes backed right up against the stockade, other buildings could be seen, many seemed permanent, others makeshift. There were even a few canvas tents. Nearby several teepees added still more variety to the scene.

A narrow stream wound its way toward the fort and passed right through its center beneath low openings in the stockade heavily guarded by barbed wire. The stream's bed was almost dry, but a thin trickle of water wandered down the middle of it, making it easy to see why the army had elected to place its outpost at this particular location in the dry west Texas country.

Of greatest interest to Shannon at the moment were a series of stock pens located near the fort. They were empty, but they were of sufficient size to hold many hundred head of cattle or horses if the need arose.

The gates of the stockade were open, and people and wagons were passing freely in and out, unmolested by the sleepy sentry who leaned against one of the gateposts, picking his teeth and staring with dull eyes out across the prairie. He straightened up as he saw Shannon and the vaqueros approaching, though, and stepped out in front of them to block the entrance to the fort.

"Halt!" the sentry bawled, holding his carbine at the ready across his chest. "Who are you and what's your business here?"

"I'm a federal marshal," Shannon said. "I want to see the commanding officer."

"Why?" the sentry asked, peering suspiciously at the badge on Shannon's shirt. "You come to arrest one of our boys?"

"If I have," Shannon replied, "I'll discuss it with your C.O. when I see him. Now, if you'll just step aside. . . ."

"Oh, awright," the sentry said reluctantly. "*You* can go in, Marshal, but them others gotta wait here. The colonel don't like Mexicans and Injuns coming inside the fort."

Shannon gathered up his reins.

"In the first place," he said evenly, "these 'Mexicans' are American citizens. And, in any case, they're with me, and they're coming in with me."

"You better not give me no trouble," the soldier exclaimed, backing away and cocking the carbine. "You mess with me and I'll call the officer of the guard."

"Then by all means call him," Shannon said, "because we're hot and tired and we're coming in even if we have to ride over top of you in the process. Any more objections?"

Before the sentry could reply, a young lieutenant appeared and asked what was going on. The sentry gestured at Shannon.

"This tin star wants to see the colonel," he said. "He wants to take these Mexes into the fort with him."

"Well, then, let them in," the lieutenant said.

"But Colonel Clinton's orders . . . ," the sentry began.

"I'll take the responsibility," the lieutenant replied. "Now uncock that piece and get back to your post."

He walked over to Shannon and reached up to shake his hand.

"Name's Trent," he said. "Welcome to Fort Lister, Marshal. Sorry about the trouble with the sentry. The colonel's touchy about strangers coming into the fort, and he's given the guards strict orders."

"Yes, I can see that," Shannon said. "Thanks for your help."

"Glad to be of service. Come on, I'll take you to the colonel."

By the time Shannon had tied his horse to the hitch rail and mounted the steps to the headquarters building, he had already decided that he was not going to like the fort's commander. In this, he was not disappointed. Clinton was a portly man of middle height and middle age. His uniform was rumpled, his hair was greasy and thin, and his puffy face bore the marks of permanent petulance. He did not rise as Lieutenant Trent ushered Shannon into his office. Trent saluted crisply; Clinton did not return the salute.

"What's this about you letting a bunch of Mexicans into the fort?" he barked at Trent as they entered. "You know my orders."

"Yes, sir," Trent replied calmly. "However, this man is a United States marshal, and the other men are with him. I didn't think. . . ."

"You aren't paid to think," Clinton barked. "You're paid to follow my orders. Well, go on back out there and keep an eye on them while I talk to this man."

He swiveled his chair around to face Shannon and eyed him with patent dislike.

"So you're a U.S. marshal, are you?" he said, snickering. "Well, what do you want here?"

There was a pot of coffee sitting on top of a woodstove a few feet away.

"Mind if I have a cup?" Shannon asked.

"Yes," the colonel snapped. "I mind."

"Then perhaps you won't object if I at least sit down," Shannon said, carefully keeping his temper. He needed this man's help, and he would do what he had to in order to get it—up to a point.

Clinton snorted.

"You don't need to sit down," he said. "You aren't going to be here that long."

Shannon sighed. It was plain that no amount of tact or diplomacy was going to elicit Clinton's help. Perhaps, he decided, a harder line would be more successful. Very deliberately, he walked over to the stove and poured himself a cup of coffee. Then he pulled up the chair that stood in front of the desk and sat down in it.

"Thank you," he said, leaning back. "I appreciate your hospitality."

"All right," Clinton said angrily. "You've got your coffee and your chair. Now, one more time—what do you want here?"

"I'm looking for a herd of cattle," Shannon said. "Two thousand head or a little less, wearing a 'Box A' brand. You don't happen to know anything about them, do you?"

"Doesn't mean anything to me," Clinton said with a sneer, avoiding Shannon's eyes. "This is an army post, not a cattle ranch."

"Perhaps I can refresh your memory," Shannon said. "They were brought here within the past two or three days by a man named Snyder. Does that ring any bells?"

Clinton's sneer became a smirk.

"Oh, yeah," he said with a careless wave of his hand. "Snyder. He's got a big cattle ranch somewhere around here. I forget where. I buy stock from him occasionally for the army and for the Indian Agency. Didn't think you meant his cattle."

"They aren't his," Shannon said. "They're mine. Or were until he stole them. He was here, then?"

Clinton picked up a swagger stick from the desk and began to tap it nervously on the desktop.

"Well, he did come through a while ago. I don't remember exactly when."

"And the cattle?"

"I bought them for the army, naturally. Kept some to feed our men and sent the rest off to the other posts and the Indian reservations, just like I always do."

His smirk broadened.

"So you see, you're a little late, Marshal," he chuckled. "The deal's done, and the cattle are gone. Sorry."

"Your deal was illegal, Colonel," Shannon replied. "The cattle were stolen, and a sale of stolen property is void under the law."

"Maybe," Clinton grinned, "but even if I still had the

cattle, all I've got for it is your word that they were stolen, and that's not good enough. Too bad, Shannon. You should have gotten here a few days sooner."

Shannon rose from the chair and leaned over Clinton's desk, placing his clenched fists firmly on the desktop.

"Your story smells like old fish, Clinton," he said. "In the first place, you know perfectly well that those cattle were stolen. You also know that Snyder's no cattle rancher—he's a thief, plain and simple, and you're in cahoots with him. Furthermore, two thousand cattle don't just disappear overnight without a trace. They're around here somewhere, and I want them back. Every last one of them."

Clinton leapt up and slammed the swagger stick down on the desktop.

"I don't care what you want, Shannon!" he bellowed. "I'm the commanding officer of this post, and I give the orders around here, so don't get smart with me or I'll have you chucked into the guardhouse along with your Mexican pals."

"I wouldn't try that if I were you," Shannon said. "Your soldiers might find my 'Mexican pals' a little hard to 'chuck.' Furthermore, if you or any of your men lay hands on me, I'll place you under arrest for obstruction of justice and assaulting a federal officer."

"Don't try to bluff me, Shannon," Clinton rasped. "You're on army property, and you don't have any jurisdiction to arrest anybody for anything here."

"Try me," Shannon said. "You might be surprised." He was tired and irritable, and this officious fool had pushed him too far. Moving slowly so that Clinton could see plainly what he was doing, Shannon slipped the rawhide loop off the hammer of his Colt and stepped back from the desk, a cold light in his eyes.

Clinton frowned and hurriedly sat down again. Shannon saw that beads of perspiration had suddenly appeared on his forehead.

"Take it easy," Clinton said, eyeing Shannon's six-gun. "There's no need for any rough stuff."

"Then let's go over it again, Colonel, step by step. One, my cattle have been stolen. Two, I want them back. Three, I expect you to help me get them back. Is that simple enough for you?"

Clinton shrugged. Now safely back behind his desk, he had resumed his arrogant manner.

"Your problems aren't my concern, Shannon," he said. "The cattle have been bought and paid for, and they've been shipped out. If you want the money I gave for them, go after the people who sold them to me. Maybe they'll share it with you. Maybe, but I doubt it."

"There's more to this than just money," Shannon said. "Snyder and his mob are wanted for larceny and murder. I'm asking for your help in finding them. If you decline to help me, as a United States marshal I'll feel obligated to inform your superiors in Washington of your lack of co-operation with civil authority. They probably wouldn't like that very much, especially if Congress got wind of it too. They might call it 'conduct unbecoming an officer' or some such thing. You wouldn't have much chance of being promoted to general with a congressional inquiry and a court-martial on your record, would you?"

Clinton seemed more alarmed by this idea than he had been by Shannon's threat to arrest him. He was perspiring again, and he took out his handkerchief and began dabbing nervously at the rivulets of moisture running down his brow.

"Oh, well, now look, Marshal," he said, his manner again conciliatory, "you've got it all wrong. If those cattle were stolen, of course I'd like to help you get them back. But they're gone, and there's nothing I can do about that. As for catching Snyder and his men, I just can't spare you any of my troopers right now."

"Why not?" Shannon said, half amused by this sudden change of tone and tactics. It was clear that his mention of Washington had struck a nerve.

"It's the Indians," Clinton said. "Yeah, that's it—the Indians. The Comanches are on the loose again, and I've got all I can handle just guarding this territory from them. Keeping the settlements around here safe from Indian raids is my responsibility. I can't abandon my duty just to worry about a few cows or a few small-time rustlers. Be reasonable."

Shannon regarded him with contempt.

"I'd almost swallow that story," he said acidly, "if I hadn't met the company of Texas Rangers, all nine of them, who are *really* guarding this territory. They're the ones who are running the risks while you sit here on your hands getting kickbacks on the purchase of stolen cattle and starving the Indians into rebellion. You make me sick, Clinton. You're a liar, a thief, and a disgrace to the uniform you wear."

The Colonel turned beet-red. His eyes bulged in fury and spittle began flying from his trembling lips.

"Get out of here, Shannon!" he screeched. "Get out of here or so help me I'll have my men shoot you down like a dog, court-martial or no court-martial!"

Shannon stared at him for a moment, debating whether or not he should slap handcuffs and leg irons on the man and duck-walk him out the gate. But his better judgment quickly overtook his anger. Clinton's troops probably despised him, but they would hardly stand idly by while their commanding officer was carted off under arrest by Shannon and the vaqueros.

"Clinton," he said calmly, "I have a great deal of respect for the U.S. Army. I've met many Army officers, and without exception they've all been people of honor and integrity. My father's older brother was a Union officer—he died at Gettysburg defending the same flag that flies in front of your headquarters. You have no place among such men. Sooner or later, the army's going to find out what a piece of slime you are and cashier you right out there on your own parade ground. When they do, I hope I'll be here to see them rip your buttons off. And I hope it happens very, very soon."

"Officer of the guard!" Clinton screamed. "Officer of the guard! Trent, get in here!"

Lieutenant Trent opened the door and walked unhurriedly in. He appeared so promptly that it seemed likely he had been listening outside the door.

"Lieutenant," Clinton shrieked, "throw this man off the post, and tell the sentries that if he ever shows up again they're to shoot him on sight."

Trent looked quizzically at Shannon.

"Never mind, Lieutenant," Shannon said. "I'm leaving."

He turned on his heel, walked out of Clinton's office, nodded pleasantly to the clerks in the orderly room, and went through the front door of the headquarters into the sunlight. Lieutenant Trent followed him onto the parade ground.

"That was worth seeing," he said admiringly. "Nobody ever talked to Clinton that way before. Well done."

"You know about him?" Shannon said.

"Oh, yes," Trent said. "*Everybody* knows about him."

"Why doesn't the army do something about him, then?"

"Well," Trent said with a smile, "as a matter of fact, the army *is* doing something. I don't think the colonel knows about it yet, but there's an inspector-general on the way here even as we speak. When the I.G. gets through with Clinton, the good colonel will be lucky to wind up as a private peeling potatoes at Fort Leavenworth. Don't worry about him, Marshal. The army will settle accounts with him. Meanwhile, you've got some cattle to find and some rustlers to catch."

"That may not be so easy, now," Shannon said. "According to Clinton, the cattle are scattered all over Texas and the rustlers are long gone."

"Maybe," Trent said, "and maybe not. Come on, let's get you and your men out the gate before the colonel changes his mind about kicking you off the post and decides to have you shot instead."

Shannon untied his horse and headed for the front gate, with Trent beside him and the vaqueros following him. When they were outside the fort, beyond earshot of the sentry, Trent turned to Shannon.

"Look, Marshal," he said, "I've just returned here from a trip to Washington, and I don't know anything firsthand about your cattle. However, I heard you talking with the colonel about that fellow Snyder. Would it help if you could find him?"

"Yes," Shannon said. "It would help a great deal. Do you know where he is?"

"No," Trent replied, "but I may be able to put you in touch with someone who does."

He guided Shannon further away from the gate and pointed along one of the stockade walls.

"There's a small cantina down there—you'll see it. Ask for a girl named Pepita Lopez. She may be able to assist you."

"Friend of Snyder's?" Shannon asked.

Trent smiled.

"In a manner of speaking," he replied cryptically. "Well," he added, holding out his hand, "I'd better be getting back. Good luck, Marshal. If the I.G. chops off Clinton's head, I'll send you his ears."

## Chapter Fourteen

They found the cantina without difficulty. Leaving the vaqueros outside to watch for trouble, Shannon and Ramón went in. The interior was lit only by the weak sunlight filtering through two dusty windows, and Shannon and Ramón paused briefly inside the door to let their eyes become accustomed to the semidarkness. Two cavalrymen were sitting at a corner table playing a desultory game of poker; otherwise the cantina appeared deserted except for the bartender. This worthy was seated on a stool behind the bar, polishing glasses with a dirty rag.

"*Buenos tardes,* Señores," he said unenthusiastically. "What will you have?"

"We would like to speak to Pepita Lopez," Ramón replied.

The bartender assumed a vacant look.

"I do not know if she is here," he said.

Shannon dropped a five-dollar gold piece on the bar.

"Perhaps you could find out for us," he suggested.

The bartender seized the coin and vanished hastily through a curtained doorway. Presently a young woman came out, leaned against the bar, and inspected them with suspicion.

"You wish to see me?" she asked.

"Yes," Shannon said. "I'm Clay Shannon, and this is my friend, Señor Ramón Peralta. Is there somewhere we could talk in private?"

As he spoke, Shannon saw that something was wrong with the girl. He could not make out her face in the dim light, but her features seemed oddly misshapen.

"Talk?" the girl said. "Just talk?"

"Yes, Señorita," said Ramón. "Do not be alarmed. We mean you no harm."

She stared at them for a moment, then shrugged.

"Come to my room," she said. "We can speak there if you wish."

The room was small and drab, and there was only one chair. The girl sat on the edge of the bed, while Shannon, at Ramón's insistence, took the chair. Ramón leaned comfortably against one wall, watching. There was an oil lamp on a stand at the head of the bed; Pepita Lopez lit it and then turned to face them. Shannon was startled to see that there was indeed something wrong with her. Both eyes were blackened and her face was swollen and covered with bruises. In addition, a deep cut, just beginning to heal, ran from the left side of her forehead across the bridge of her nose and down her right cheek to her jaw. Shannon struggled to conceal his shock. The girl was now gazing dully at him, waiting. He forced a smile and leaned forward toward her.

"We need your help, Señorita," he said. "We're looking for a man named Snyder. Do you know him?"

The girl's face paled.

"You—you are a friend of his?" Her voice quavered.

Shannon thought quickly. If he gave the wrong answer, she probably would not tell them anything. He decided that the best course would be to answer truthfully.

"No," he said. "We're not friends of his. Quite the contrary."

"Then why do you wish to find him?"

This time Shannon did not hesitate.

"To hang him, I hope," he said.

The girl uttered a chilling laugh.

"Excellent," she said. "I would like to see him hanged."

"Why?" Shannon asked, already guessing the answer.

Pepita pointed to her face.

"This is why," she said. "He beat me and then cut me with his knife. I am eighteen years old, Señor, and my beauty is gone forever. I am a freak now, and no man will touch me. I may starve because of him."

She began to cry.

Shannon always felt awkward around sobbing women, but for all his hardness and the violence of his life, he was in many ways a kind man, and seeing her grief he reached out and touched her shoulder gently.

"Do not distress yourself, Señorita," he said. "You are strong, and when the bruises are gone you will still be beautiful." He knew that it was not true, but for some reason he felt a sudden tenderness toward the disfigured girl, and a new wave of hatred for Snyder.

"Why did this man hurt you?" Ramón asked, equally incensed.

"He asks for me whenever he is at the fort," she said, drying her eyes with a small handkerchief. "I despise him, and this time I refused to go with him. He became very angry and beat me senseless. When I regained consciousness, I was as you see me now."

"Didn't anyone try to help you?" Shannon asked indignantly.

The girl gave a wan smile.

"Who would help the likes of me?" she said sadly.

"*I'll* help you," Shannon said, "if I can. But first I must ask you to help me. When did Snyder do this to you?"

"Two nights ago. He left the next day."

"Do you know where he's gone?"

"He has a small *rancho* about thirty miles from here. He uses it to hold stolen cattle until he can sell them. I think he may have gone there."

"Did he have any cattle with him this time?"

"Some, yes. He sold them to the fat colonel at the fort. But he probably had many more nearby, out of sight. He has an arrangement with the colonel—the colonel pays for many animals, but takes only a few. Snyder gives the colonel back part of the money, then takes the rest of the cattle to his ranch and sells them again to someone else. He shares that money with the colonel too."

*What a lovely scheme,* Shannon thought. *Snyder and our friend the colonel get rich on the government's money and other people's cattle. That inspector general is going to have apoplexy when he finds out about this.*

"What is it that you say?" the girl asked.

"Nothing," Shannon replied. "Is Snyder coming back here soon?"

"I do not know, Señor. I do not think so. That last evening when he was very drunk he told me that someone would be coming to his *rancho* soon with more stolen cattle, and that he would have to wait there for them until they arrived."

"This ranch of Snyder's—can you take me there?"

The girl's eyes widened in fright.

"Oh, no," she said. "I could not do that. I am leaving this place soon and going far away to try to find work and make a new life for myself. If I led you to that pig, and he learned about it, he would do something terrible to me."

"No," Shannon said, "you're wrong there. He won't harm you. Once I get my hands on him, he's going to be too busy dancing at the end of a rope to harm anybody else, ever again."

"You give me your word that you will not let him hurt me?" the girl said, looking thoughtful.

"Yes."

"And you will kill him when you find him?"

"If I have to. I'd prefer to take him back to New Mexico to hang, but if I cannot, then yes, I will kill him."

A ghastly smile twisted Pepita's marred features.

"Then I will lead you to him," she said. "And if you do not kill him, I will."

## Chapter Fifteen

They rode in silence, covering the miles steadily with Shannon and Ramón in the lead and Pepita Lopez beside them. Shannon had purchased a horse for the girl at the fort, but she sat awkwardly in the saddle and Shannon thought sympathetically of the aches and pains that she, like anyone unaccustomed to long hours on horseback, would have by the time they arrived at Snyder's hideout.

They reached it at midday. Pepita warned them when they were still well short of the place, and they went forward cautiously, watching for guards and making as little noise as possible. Here and there they passed stray steers wandering in the brush, and Shannon noticed with grim amusement that they bore a variety of brands, some of which were his own.

Finally, at Pepita's suggestion, they dismounted and proceeded on foot through some broken country to the edge of a high bluff. Looking down, they saw that the little valley below them held a large number of cattle, perhaps a thousand head or more. Even at that distance Shannon could see that most of them bore the "Box A" brand of Rancho Alvarez.

*Only a thousand or so,* Shannon mused. *Snyder must have already disposed of the rest. Well, at least I'll get half of our herd back.*

In the center of the valley, a weathered shack sat next to a delapidated corral. Smoke curled from the house's chimney, and Shannon counted six horses in the corral.

Shannon and his men concealed themselves in the rocks along the rim of the valley and watched keenly for a time as the cattle milled about. Several riders were moving around the herd, keeping it together.

"I count five herders," said Ramón at length. "And seven horses in the corral. Unless the horses are just part of the their remuda, we could have as many as a dozen *banditos* to deal with."

"Yes," Shannon said, "plus others that we may not have seen yet."

"A formidable task for our little band," said Ramón. "Shall we attack now?"

Shannon pondered the question. If they went charging down into the herd in broad daylight, they would be facing an unknown number of guns, some of which would be firing at them from the shelter of the house. On the other hand, they could wait until nightfall, but with the herd surrounding the house and the night herders moving about on all sides, their chances of achieving surprise were almost nonexistent. He found himself wishing that he had not lost so many men during the journey to this place. Their presence would have improved the odds considerably. Furthermore, had someone other than Colonel Clinton been in command at Fort Lister, he might have a troop of cavalry with him now instead of just a few tired vaqueros. Well, there was no help for it. There were no more vaqueros and no troop of cavalry, and there was no point in wishing. They were alone, a handful of men and a girl, and they faced a formidable task, with the odds against success—or even survival—very high indeed.

But Shannon had not come all that long way to be defeated by last-minute difficulties. The cattle below him belonged to Rancho Alvarez, to Charlotte, and to him, and he would have them back regardless of the odds. A plan was needed, and he set himself to work one out.

Then a thought struck him.

"Señorita Lopez," he said, "you mentioned that Snyder told you he was expecting someone else to come here with more cattle. Did he say when they were due?"

"No, Señor, but I think it was soon—perhaps only a few days."

"What do you have in mind, *Patrón?*" Ramón asked.

"Those strays we passed coming in here. What if we rounded up some of them and then came riding down into the valley with them, as if we were the ones Snyder was waiting for? If we're lucky, we might get right up close to the house before they realize that we're not the people they were expecting."

"An excellent idea," Ramón said. "But—forgive me for asking, *Patrón*—what if the men and cattle they were waiting for have already arrived?"

"Then," Shannon said, looking him right in the eye, "we will probably never leave the valley alive."

Ramón considered this for a moment, then smiled.

"I'll take the men and go collect the strays," he said. "We will be as quick as we can."

Shannon grinned.

"Good," he said. "Miss Lopez and I will wait here and watch. And don't worry—we won't start the fun without you."

It took the vaqueros nearly an hour to assemble enough cattle to present the appearance of a small herd. When they were finally ready, Shannon held a brief council of war.

"We'll ride down there pushing the herd ahead of us," he explained. "We'll take the cattle as close in to the house as we can before the shooting starts. Keep your hats low and try to avoid eye contact with any of the herders we pass. And be ready, because if they recognize us or realize that we're not the people they're expecting, things could get nasty very quickly."

He turned to the girl.

"Señorita," he said, "you remain up here. Keep yourself and your horse out of sight. I plan to win this fight, but if things go badly for us, get on your horse and ride away as hard as you can and as far as you can. Here, take this."

He handed her a small leather bag filled with gold coins.

"This should take care of you for awhile at least," he said. "Thank you for your help. May God go with you."

"And with you, Señores," she replied. There were tears in her eyes, and Shannon could see the fear on her face.

"Don't worry," he told her. "I've never lost a gunfight yet, and I don't intend to start now." He looked away, wishing that he felt as confident of the outcome as his words to her indicated.

Carefully he unpinned the U.S. marshal's badge from his shirt and slipped it into his pocket.

"Just this once, we'll hide the badge," he said, grinning at Ramón. He buttoned the flap of the pocket, then turned to the waiting vaqueros.

"Ready, *muchachos?*" he called. They murmured their fierce assent. "Then," Shannon said, "let us go down among our enemies and teach them the lesson they deserve. Good luck to all of you, my friends."

*"Buena suerte, Patrón,"* they replied, gathering up their reins. Their eagerness for battle showed plainly in their manner and on their faces. Shannon reflected that if he were to die that day, he could not die in better company.

Slowly they started down the trail into the valley, driving the small herd of strays ahead of them. Shannon rode in front with his hat pulled well down over his eyes to delay the possibility that one of the rustlers might recognize him before they reached the shack. As they came over the hill, the herders all reined up and stared warily at them, and two of them drew their rifles from their saddle scabbards. The nearest herder came riding over to Shannon, suspicion on his face. Shannon was relieved to see that the man was a stranger to him, someone he had never met before and who therefore was unlikely to recognize him as an enemy.

"You the people we been waitin' for?" the man asked in a sullen manner.

*What a stupid question,* Shannon thought. *What would the fool expect me to say—"No?"*

"Yeah," he said gruffly. "Where's Snyder?"

"He's in the house," the herder replied. "Tell your men to run this bunch in with the others. We want to get 'em started for the railroad as soon as we can. We been hangin' around this hole in the ground for a coupla days waitin' for you."

"You heard the man," Shannon called to the vaqueros. He kept his tone careless for the benefit of the listening rustlers. "Put 'em in with the rest. Then come on over to the house, and we'll see if we can scare up some grub. Come on, Ramón. I want to talk to Snyder."

This little speech seemed to arouse no suspicion among the herders, who began to help push the new cattle in with the remainder of the herd. Shannon and Ramón rode toward the house. As they did so, three men came out onto the porch, watching them as they approached. They were all carrying coffee cups, and one of them was rubbing the sleep out of his eyes. None of them seemed suspicious or apprehensive.

"These people are loco," Ramón said out of the corner of his mouth. "They post no guards and they take no precautions when strangers ride in. They are very ignorant men. One wonders how they have survived so long."

"Well," Shannon said in a low voice, "they're about to get educated. Be ready, though, because when Snyder comes out, he'll recognize us immediately."

"Hey, boss," one of the men on the porch called over his shoulder. "We got company."

Snyder walked out onto the porch, looking surly.

"Where the devil you been?" he grumbled. "We been waitin' for you for. . . ."

He stopped abruptly, his eyes wide.

"Shannon!" he gasped. "It's the law, boys! Gun 'em down!"

Shannon had noted before that whenever he was involved in gunplay, time seemed to become distorted. It was as if for a few moments he was viewing everything in slow motion. He knew full well that just the opposite was true, that in most gunfights everything happened in a few split seconds, but while a battle was in progress he always felt as if the passage of time was suddenly suspended, and he was moving through the confrontation one step at a time, as if in a terrible dream. This occasion was no exception.

Snyder went for his six-gun. The other men on the porch dropped their coffee cups and followed suit. But surprise had hindered their reflexes, and Shannon had the Colt in his hand before the first cup hit the floor of the porch. As usual, Snyder was the slowest on the draw, and so Shannon's first shot was directed at the man on Snyder's left, whose revolver was just clearing its holster. The Colt roared, and the outlaw went over backwards, Shannon's bullet in his chest. Shannon swung the muzzle of the Colt toward the other two men and killed one of them; as he did so, Ramón's first shot knocked the third man to his knees. Snyder had by now managed to yank his revolver from its holster, and was raising it to shoot at Shannon.

"Drop it, Snyder!" Shannon said, holding his fire. "You're under arrest!"

Snyder pulled the trigger, but in his haste and panic the bullet went far above Shannon's head. With an oath Snyder fled back through the door of the house and slammed it shut.

"You did not kill him?" Ramón asked, surprised.

"No," Shannon said. "I want him alive."

The rest of the startled outlaws had now grasped the fact that they were not among friends, and had begun to shoot at the Alvarez men. The vaqueros returned fire, then charged forward, shouting defiance. The rustlers, unnerved by this sudden assault, loosed one more volley and then turned to flee, dashing through the startled cattle as they tried to escape. One by one, they went down as the vaqueros overtook them.

The glass of one of the shack's windows shattered, and a revolver barrel pushed through the broken pane as Snyder opened fire at Shannon and Ramón.

"Keep me covered, Ramón!" Shannon shouted over the noise of the gunfire. He slid out of the saddle and leapt up onto the porch, then kicked with all his might at the rickety door. The hinges gave way, and the splintered door went flying into the house with Shannon right behind it.

As he dove through the door, Shannon threw himself to the floor and then scrambled hastily out of the square of light from the now-open doorway. Snyder was shooting at him, but in the outlaw's panic his shots went wild. Shannon pulled over the table that stood in the middle of the room and crouched behind it, waiting. As he had anticipated, the next time Snyder pulled the trigger of the revolver nothing happened. Snyder had fired six shots, and the weapon was now empty.

Snarling, Snyder fumbled at his belt for more ammunition. Shannon shoved the table aside and rushed directly at the outlaw, ramming his shoulder into Snyder's midsection, knocking the breath out of him, and slamming him to the floor. Gasping for air, Snyder came to his feet and hurled the empty revolver at Shannon's head. Shannon ducked and the revolver sailed past him to bounce with a loud clang off the woodstove behind him.

"Give it up, Snyder!" Shannon called, leveling his six-gun. "Don't make me kill you!"

Snyder uttered another expletive and tried to dash past Shannon toward the open door. Shannon raised the Colt and smashed it against Snyder's head as the outlaw went past. Snyder cartwheeled into the wall, dazed but still conscious. A chair stood against the wall, and Snyder scrambled up and seized it. He raised it high above his head and came at Shannon again, his face contorted with fear and hate. Shannon sidestepped the swinging chair and drove his fist against Snyder's jaw. Snyder threw up his arms, and the chair went flying out through the half-broken window, smashing the remainder of the panes. Shannon hit him again, driving a hard right against the bridge of Snyder's nose. Snyder staggered backwards into a corner, hung for a moment against the wall, and then slid slowly to the floor, his eyes glazed over. Shannon walked over to him and pulled him roughly to his feet.

"Like I said, Snyder," Shannon said, "you're under arrest."

Snyder shook his head to clear it, then shrieked another curse and tried to twist out of Shannon's grasp. Shannon spun the outlaw around, drew back his fist, and hit him full in the face as hard as he could. Propelled by the force of the blow, Snyder tumbled backwards out the door of the shack, then rolled across the porch and off it into the dirt beyond. This time he made no attempt to get up but merely lay there in the dust, whimpering.

Shannon followed him out onto the porch and looked around. The vaqueros had overwhelmed the remainder of Snyder's men and were tying up the survivors. Ramón was bending over the third man who had been on the porch with Snyder, examining his wound.

"This one's alive, more or less," he said. "The other two are dead. Are you all right, *Patrón?*"

Shannon stepped off the porch into the sunlight and looked up at the clear, blue sky.

"Yes," he said softly. "Yes, I am."

He looked at Ramón and then at the other vaqueros.

"Did we lose anyone?"

"I think not, Señor," Ramón said. "Porfirio has a slight wound in his leg, but everyone else is unharmed. They didn't put up much of a fight, did they?"

Shannon felt his bruised knuckles and looked down at Snyder, who was now moving feebly in the dirt.

"Not much," he said. "Not enough of one, anyway."

Ramón bent over Snyder and began tying his hands and feet.

"That hurts!" Snyder moaned as the knots were pulled tight.

*"Sí,"* Ramón said. "I know."

Pepita Lopez came riding down the slope and brought her horse to a stop near the porch.

*"Magnifico!"* she said, looking around at the vaqueros, who were trussing up the surviving rustlers. "You have won, Señor, as you said you would."

Then she saw Snyder squirming on the ground, and her face darkened. She slid off the horse and looked down at him, her eyes bright with hatred.

"But this pig is still alive!" she said, looking reproachfully at Shannon.

"Yes," Shannon replied, "but when I get him back to Santa Fe, a jury will remedy that situation very quickly."

Pepita, obviously displeased, stared at the prostrate Snyder for a long moment, breathing heavily. Then she uttered a scream of hate and leaped toward the defenseless outlaw. A knife appeared in her hand as she straddled Snyder's body and ripped open his shirt. Shannon sprang forward and seized her wrist just as the blade started to descend toward Snyder's bared chest.

"Hold it, Señorita," Shannon said, gripping her arm tightly. "This man is my prisoner."

"But you said you would kill him!" she protested.

"No, little one," Shannon responded. "I said I would kill him *if I had to*. He's under arrest now, and he'll be taken back to New Mexico to be tried and hanged. Let me have the knife."

He pried the weapon gently from her fingers and handed it to Ramón. The girl stared at him, distraught.

"Please, Señor Shannon," she said tearfully, "let me cut out his heart. You can hang the rest of him when you get back to New Mexico."

"Sorry, *muchacha*," Shannon said. "Let the law take care of him. It's better that way. Besides," he added with a wry smile, "you don't want him to have a quick death, do you? Hanging is slower and much more painful."

Pepita looked doubtful.

"You are sure he will suffer?" she asked. "A great deal, I mean?"

"I think you'll be satisfied with the results," Shannon said, awed by the fierceness of her wrath. *Eighteen years old,* he thought, *and she's already built up enough hatred for a lifetime. You ought to thank me, Snyder. I'm a much less fearsome adversary than this girl.*

He propelled her gently away from Snyder and into Ramón's grasp.

"Hold onto her, will you?" he said to the chief vaquero. "I want to see what shape the rest of these rattlesnakes are in."

## Chapter Sixteen

There was much work to be done, and the Alvarez men set about it wearily but with grim satisfaction. There were several dead rustlers to be buried, but curiously there were no wounded. Shannon noted that a few of the dead outlaws had suffered knife wounds after they had been shot, but he did not think it wise to question the vaqueros too closely about this. The vaqueros made certain the surviving rustlers were securely bound and placed in a row along the front wall of the shack, then they began to round up the cattle that had been scattered during the gunfight.

Shannon and Ramón searched the outlaws' pockets and then went through the house, finding several items that had belonged to the vaqueros who were murdered when the herd was stolen. Finally, hidden behind one of the bunks, they discovered a canvas pouch marked "U.S. Army." Inside the pouch was a large sum of money in gold coins and a crumpled receipt for the sale of one thousand eight hundred and twenty-two cattle. The receipt was signed by Col. Percival Clinton, U.S. Army.

"Well, well," Shannon mused, looking at the document. "I think I'll send this along to that inspector general who's coming to Fort Lister. He should find it most interesting."

"You will keep the gold, of course?" Ramón said.

"No," Shannon said. "It will have to be returned to the army."

He placed the coins and the receipt back into the canvas pouch and handed it to Ramón.

"Here," he said. "Have one of our men deliver this in person to Lieutenant Trent at the fort. He'll know what to do with it."

"But it is your money, Señor," Ramón objected. "You have lost over a thousand head of cattle, and this is the gold that the outlaws got for them."

"It's stolen money, Ramón," Shannon said. "I can't keep it. When we determine how many head Snyder actually sold at the fort, the government will pay me for them."

He glanced at the row of tied-up outlaws in front of the shack.

"Besides," he added, "I really don't care much about the money. What I want now is justice. That's more important than money—and much harder to find these days."

When the remaining cattle had been rounded up, Shannon gathered the vaqueros around him.

"Now, my friends," he said, "it's time to go home. Ramón, you take the cattle and herd them back to the Pecos. Bring them to the crossing upstream from Casa Cochina, and wait for me there. With so few head left, you should have enough men to drive them that far without too much difficulty."

"And the *banditos?*" Ramón asked. "Surely we should hang them here, instead of taking them all the way back to New Mexico."

"Now you're starting to sound like Señorita Lopez," Shannon said with a laugh, trying to deflect the men's anger. But the vaqueros were in no mood for humor. They growled in agreement with Ramón, and one of them unhooked his rope from his saddle, hefting it and looking suggestively at the trussed-up rustlers. Shannon saw that he was on the verge of having a small mutiny on his hands, one that might prove fatal for Snyder and his friends.

"Listen to me, *amigos*," he said. "As much as I'd like to string them up right here and be done with it, I can't. This won't let me." He removed the U.S. marshal's badge from his pocket and held it up for all to see. "I'm sworn to uphold the law, and the law says that these men must be tried for their crimes by a judge and jury. Have no fear, they'll hang, but only when and where the law says they should. That's the way of all law-abiding people. It's our way, my friends, yours and mine. Otherwise we're no better than the men we hang, and I don't want to descend to their level."

The vaqueros nodded reluctantly in agreement.

"Good," Shannon said, pinning the badge back on his shirt. "Now let's get ready to move. It'll be slow going with the cattle, so I'll ride on ahead. I'm anxious about

Doña Carlotta, and wish to rejoin her as soon as possible. Ramón, I'll need to take a couple of men to help me haul Snyder and his henchmen back to Casa Cochina. Once we get there, Marshal Casey will let us borrow his jail for a few days until we're ready to move north again."

"When we reach Casa Cochina, *Patrón,* what then?" Ramón asked.

"If Señora Shannon is able to travel by the time you arrive with the cattle, we'll all head for Rancho Alvarez together. If not, you can take the herd on to the ranch and the bandits to the jail in Los Santos. I'll wait in Casa Cochina until the Señora is well enough to be moved. Then I'll bring her home, pick up Snyder and his friends from the Los Santos jail, and take them to Santa Fe for trial. Is that clear? Then let's begin. We have another long journey ahead of us."

"Señor?" said a small voice, and Shannon realized that he had forgotten about Pepita Lopez.

"Señor," she said, "*por favor,* may I go with you? I can cook for your men. I am a very good cook, and I can help with the other work also."

Shannon thought for a moment. Certainly Pepita would be no worse off in Casa Cochina than she was now, alone in the middle of west Texas.

"Very well, little one," he said. "You can go with Ramón and the vaqueros while they move the herd northward. Ramón, look after her, will you? I rely on you to see that she reaches Casa Cochina safely."

"*Si, Patrón,*" Ramón said, grinning. "It will be nice for a change to have something to eat besides cold beans and jerky."

## Chapter Seventeen

There were eight surviving rustlers, and their addition to the Casa Cochina jail strained Marshal Casey's facilities to bursting. Casey locked the last of the cell doors and then came into the outer office where Shannon was waiting.

"I won't be able to arrest anybody until you get those birds out of there," he said good-humoredly.

Shannon's smile was thin. The strain of bringing the prisoners north with so few men to watch them had taken its toll, and he was very tired.

"Have you seen your wife yet?" Casey continued. "She's staying at the home of Doc Peterson and his wife."

"How is she?" Shannon asked anxiously. He had received no word about Charlotte since he had started into Texas many days before, and he was very worried about her.

"She's fine," Casey said. "A little weak still, but she's been up and around for a couple of days. She's fretting about you, though. You were right—I practically had to put her in the calaboose to keep her from going after you."

The reunion with Charlotte was warm and joyous. Once again Shannon realized with awe how much Charlotte meant to him. Life without her would be unthinkable, and he was greatly relieved to see that she was recovering fully from her wound.

One of her arms was in a sling to relieve the pressure on her injured side, but she reached out with her other hand and clasped his tightly.

"Come," she said. "As horrible as Casa Cochina is, there are some nice things about it. I've found a place where one can walk along the river. Let's go there where we can be alone. I want to hear everything that's happened."

They strolled beside the river each day after that, hand in hand as they spoke of all that lay behind, and of all that lay ahead.

"We're short a few cattle," Shannon said. "I hope the price of beef holds up until we sell the rest of the herd."

"We've lost a few old friends too," Charlotte said wistfully. "Nothing can ever make up for that."

"No," Shannon replied somberly. "But there will be justice for those who died. That I guarantee you."

Three days later Ramón and the rest of the vaqueros arrived with the cattle. Shannon introduced Pepita Lopez to Charlotte, and told her about the girl's role in the capture of Snyder and his band. The bruises on Pepita's face had receded, but the scar was still livid across her forehead and cheek.

"What will you do now, Pepita?" Charlotte asked. "Casa Cochina is not a very good place for a young girl."

Pepita lowered her eyes.

"I will find something to do," she said. "I will not go back to what I was before, but Ramón says I am a fine cook, so perhaps someone here will give me work of that sort."

"You know, Clay," Charlotte said to Shannon with a twinkle in her eye, "we have so many mouths to feed at home that our cook is often overworked. Do you think that Pepita might want to come with us back to Rancho Alvarez and help out in the kitchen?"

"I don't know," Shannon said, hiding a grin. "That's up to Pepita."

"Oh, Señora, Señor!" Pepita cried. "Is it true? Would you let me come to your *hacienda* and work for you?"

"I think it can be arranged," Shannon said. "Meanwhile, you can help care for Señora Shannon as we travel north. Her injury isn't healed completely yet, and your assistance would be much appreciated."

Pepita hurried away to tell Ramón and the others of her good fortune. When she had gone, Shannon smiled affectionately at Charlotte.

"You have a kind heart, madam," he said to her. "As everyone knows."

"Your heart is as kind as mine." Charlotte laughed. "You just hide it better than I do."

She glanced at the departing Pepita.

"I hope she will be all right," she said. "She is only a child, really. We must take good care of her."

Shannon laughed.

"That 'child' keeps a large knife under her skirt," he said, "and she knows how to use it. Don't worry about her, my dear. Believe me, if the occasion arises, Pepita Lopez can take care of herself very nicely."

Shannon had bought two wagons for the trip back to Rancho Alvarez. One would be used as a chuck wagon and would carry their food and supplies. The other would serve as an ambulance so that Charlotte could make the journey in relative comfort, for she was not yet quite able to ride a horse. On the evening before their departure, Shannon inspected the wagons and reviewed all of the preparations for the trip. Then, just as the sun was setting, he went down to the city marshal's office to say goodbye to Pat Casey.

Casey was lighting the lamp in the office when Shannon walked in.

"We'll be off in the morning," Shannon said. "I'll be by early with several men to pick up Snyder and his friends."

"I'll be glad to be rid of them," Casey said. "Nasty bunch. I'm glad I don't have to ride herd on them all the way to Los Santos. Be careful with them, Clay. I'm surprised you got them this far without them trying something."

"It's hard to try anything when you're slung facedown over the back of a horse with your hands tied underneath the animal's belly," Shannon said. "They didn't enjoy the trip, but it was peaceful for the rest of us."

Casey laughed.

"Well," he said, "a good journey to you and all of your people. Will you be back this way anytime soon?"

"I don't know," Shannon replied. "I might have some unfinished business at Fort Lister. Otherwise I doubt I'll be coming this far south again—unless of course somebody steals more of our cattle."

"That reminds me," Casey said, "Snyder has been asking to see you. Something he wants to say to you, apparently. Shall I tell him to wait until morning and say it on the trail?"

"No, it's all right. I'll talk to him now."

Casey let Shannon into the cell block and waited alertly as Shannon walked over to the cell in which Snyder was sitting.

"What's so important that it couldn't wait until tomorrow?" Shannon said. "We'll be seeing you about sunup anyway."

Snyder glared at him, his narrow-set eyes bright with malice.

"Shannon," he hissed, "I'm going to kill you. If it's the last thing I ever do, I'm going to kill you."

"It's been tried," Shannon said mildly. "In fact, you've tried it a couple of times yourself without much luck. Why bother to warn me now?"

"I want you to be thinking about it," Snyder said. "About what I'll do to you and your wife when I get the chance."

"Big talk for a man who's going to be dangling at the end of a rope in a few weeks," Shannon said.

"I ain't hung yet," Snyder snarled. "Not by a long shot."

"Understand this," Shannon said carefully. "You're going north just the way you rode in here—upside down on your horse with six or seven rifles pointed at you every minute. If you give me the slightest trouble on the trail, if I see the slightest indication that you're even *thinking* about giving me trouble, I'll turn you over to the vaqueros for a little fun and games. You're not too popular with them, I'm afraid. They wanted to string you up before, and if I give you to them while we're on the way to Los Santos, hanging's the best you can expect. So you'd better make up your mind to being a good boy for the next few days, because otherwise you won't live to see Santa Fe."

Snyder spat on the floor of the cell.

"We'll see," he said. "Yeah, we'll see."

Shannon and Charlotte had one final dinner with the doctor and his wife. Charlotte's face was still pale, but she sat at the dinner table without noticeable discomfort, chatting with the Petersons.

"I owe you both a great deal," Charlotte said to them. "You've been wonderful to me. Doctor Peterson, if you ever decide to move your practice to Los Santos, I can guarantee you many patients. Our doctor is getting on in years, and we could use your skills there."

Peterson laughed.

"Thank you, Mrs. Shannon," he said, "but I'm needed here too. The town's a bit wild, but we've friends here now and I've developed a little specialty in gunshot and knife wounds. There seem to be a lot of them in Casa Cochina. Ah, here's dessert."

Mrs. Peterson had somehow contrived to produce a quantity of ice cream for their farewell meal, and Shannon was looking forward to it. Ice cream was not often seen at Rancho Alvarez, and Charlotte had asked Mrs. Peterson for the recipe, which she had gladly given.

Shannon had just picked up his spoon to begin eating his portion when he stopped abruptly. From the distance, the sound of gunfire could be clearly heard.

"Speaking of gunshot wounds," Mrs. Peterson said resignedly, "it sounds as if my husband will be working late again."

The doctor started to reply, and then a half dozen more shots echoed in the night. Shannon arose from his chair and tossed his napkin aside.

"That's coming from the direction of the jail," he said.

His gunbelt was hanging on a peg by the front door, and he seized it as he went out. Buckling it on, he broke into a run, headed for the marshal's office. He had gone only a few yards when a man appeared out of the gloom, hurrying toward him.

"Marshal Shannon!" the man said. "There's trouble at the jail! Big trouble!"

He started to say something more, but Shannon brushed

past him and hurried on. He did not have to be told what
the trouble was.

As he approached the jail, he drew his Colt and held it
at the ready. Rounding the last corner, he saw that a man
was sprawled on the boardwalk in front of the marshal's
office. Shannon moved cautiously toward him, watching
the street and the door to the office for signs of danger.

The man lying on the boardwalk was one of Casey's
deputies, and he was bleeding from a wound in the calf.

"What happened?" Shannon asked urgently.

"Snyder and his pals busted out," the deputy said, grim-
acing in pain. "Pat and Sam are after them."

Doctor Peterson arrived carrying his bag, and Shannon
pointed to the door of the office.

"The deputy's been wounded, Doc," Shannon told him,
"and there's another man inside who may need help."

More shots could be heard now. They were coming from
the west edge of town. Shannon vaulted off the boardwalk
and ran toward the sound.

As he reached the outskirts, he could see someone in the
middle of the street bending over another man who was
lying on the ground. Shannon cocked the six-gun, unsure
of the men's identity. Then he saw that the man on the
ground was Pat Casey, and that his other deputy stood over
him.

The deputy was muttering and trying to get a bandana
around Casey's thigh.

"Who's that?" Casey said, raising his pistol and peering
at Shannon in the dim light.

Shannon quickly identified himself. Casey lowered his pistol and leaned back on his elbow, staring with disgust at his bleeding leg.

"Confound it, Clay," he said, "every time you come to town I lose some blood. I guess I deserve it, though. That's the second time Snyder has gotten away from me."

"Which way did they go?" Shannon asked, trying to contain his anger and frustration.

Casey waved at the street leading out of town.

"They started off in that direction, but that's the best I can tell you," he said, frowning in exasperation. "They must have had some horses waiting for them out here in the dark. They jumped aboard and hotfooted it away before we could even get close to them. We threw some lead in their direction, but then one of them winged me and that was the last I saw of them. Sam, did you see which way they rode after I went down?"

"Couldn't tell," the deputy said. "I stopped to see if you were all right, and when I looked up they were gone. It sounded like they were headed west, but it's hard to be sure."

A crowd had gathered, and Shannon grabbed the arm of the nearest man.

"Do you know where the Alvarez outfit is camped, out by the river?"

The man nodded.

"Good. Send someone out there to tell my foreman what's happened. Tell him I said to get the vaqueros mounted and to ride in here as quickly as he can."

He turned to Casey.

"Will you be all right, Pat?" he asked.

"Yeah, I'll be okay," Casey replied. "Sam will look after me. What are you going to do?"

"I'm going after them."

"Don't do it, Clay," Casey said, alarmed. "You'll be alone, on foot, and in the dark. They'll bushwhack you sure."

But Shannon was already gone, running into the night, looking about him for some sign of the fleeing outlaws. For many minutes he hurried on, searching the darkness and praying for a miracle, but none was forthcoming. Snyder and his men had made good on their promise to escape.

Ramón and the vaqueros arrived as Shannon was walking back toward the spot where Casey had fallen. Sam, the deputy, explained to them what had occurred, and Ramón was about to go looking for Shannon when he reappeared. Shannon sent the vaqueros after the fugitives, but he knew it would be futile. In the darkness there would be no chance whatever of catching them, or even finding their trail. Soon the vaqueros returned empty-handed, and Shannon enlisted their aid in getting the wounded Casey back to his office, where Doctor Peterson was still ministering to the injured deputy and the pistol-whipped jailer. They put the marshal on the bunk in the office and watched silently as the doctor examined his wound.

"It's not too bad, Pat," he said. "The bullet missed the artery."

Casey looked up at Shannon sheepishly.

"I'm sorry about this, Clay," he said. "Have my people told you how it happened?"

Shannon nodded. He had been questioning the wounded deputy and the old jailer while Doctor Peterson was assisting Marshal Casey, and what he had heard did not please him. While Casey and his deputy Sam were at dinner, two men charged into the office, shot the other deputy, and knocked the jailer senseless. The deputy had remained conscious and had watched helplessly as the two intruders had taken the keys, unlocked the cell doors, and let out Snyder and the others.

"They got guns from the rack on the wall," the deputy said to Shannon, "and ran out laughing like crazy. Before Snyder left, he came over to me where I was lying on the floor and kicked me in the ribs as hard as he could. Then he took off too. He left you a message, though."

"A message?" Shannon said. "What was it?"

"He said, 'Tell Shannon I'll be seeing him soon.' "

"That's all?"

"Yeah. I got my six-gun off the floor and tried to follow them, but I couldn't get to my feet. Leg's busted, I guess, where they plugged me. I crawled out onto the walk and fired a couple of shots to attract some attention, and that's where you found me."

Shannon related all this to Marshal Casey while Doctor Peterson completed his bandaging of Casey's bullet wound.

"I feel like a fool, letting them get away like that," said Casey unhappily.

"It's not your fault, Pat," Shannon said. "It looks as if we missed a couple of the gang back there in Texas. Maybe it was the men Snyder was waiting for, the ones who were bringing in more cattle. Anyway, they must have followed us and jumped your people when they saw their chance."

"Well," Casey said angrily, "as soon as Doc finishes pestering me, I'll get together everybody in Casa Cochina who's still sober at this hour, and we'll go after them. You want to come along?"

Shannon wanted very badly to go along. To lose Snyder now after all they had gone through to catch him was infuriating, and he longed to ride after the outlaws before they escaped completely. But he knew that it would be a long chase at best—with no cattle to slow them down, Snyder and his men would be putting many miles between themselves and Casa Cochina, and capturing them could be a matter of weeks or even months. West Texas was a vast place in which to hide, and they might well even head for the Mexican border and lose themselves forever in the mountains of Chihuahua, beyond the reach of U.S. law.

"You can bet your last dollar I'd like to go," Shannon said, "but I'll have to leave this one to you. I want to get my wife out of Casa Cochina and back to our home, and besides, I don't have enough men to hold those cattle here indefinitely. Recapturing Snyder will have to wait. We'll leave in the morning as planned."

"I'll try to get them, Clay," Casey said fervently. "I owe you that. And I've got a score to settle with Snyder myself, now."

Shannon nodded. He knew that Casey would do his best, but the old marshal had only one unwounded deputy, and the posse of semi-inebriated residents of Casa Cochina that he would enlist would soon tire of the chase and turn back. Eventually Casey would have no choice but to return himself, for he could not leave Casa Cochina without a marshal for very long.

"I appreciate it, Pat," Shannon said, not wanting to hurt Casey's feelings by pointing all this out to him. "If you don't catch up with them, then after I've gotten Charlotte and the herd back to Rancho Alvarez I'll return here with some federal deputies and we'll go after him together."

Casey laughed ruefully.

"Thanks for being polite," he said, "but you and I both know that by then Snyder will be in Mexico or California or maybe on the moon. He's gone, and it's my fault."

He lay back on the bunk, and when he spoke again he sounded very tired.

"You know, Clay," he said sadly, "no matter how good a lawman you've been, sooner or later the years catch up with you. Your hand slows down and your eyes grow dim, and then it's time to take the star off your shirt and look for some other line of work. I think I've reached that point. A lot of lawmen don't know when to quit, but I think that for me, 'when' is now."

Shannon forced himself to smile.

"Nonsense," he said. "You're as good as you ever were. Don't let those gray hairs of yours fool you."

But even as he said it, he knew that what Casey had said was true, and he wondered if he himself would have the sense to recognize when the time had come. *On a night like this,* he said to himself wearily, *'when' seems very near indeed.*

## Chapter Eighteen

The sun was rising over the hills across the river as Shannon helped Charlotte into the wagon he had bought for her. He watched while Pepita Lopez settled her on the bed of blankets they had put into the back for her to lie upon.

"This is silly, Clay," Charlotte protested. "I can ride up front on the seat. I'm not an invalid anymore."

"Keep her quiet, Pepita," Shannon said to the girl. "If she tries to get up, hit her with a frying pan or something."

Ramón was sitting on his horse close by, waiting for Shannon to give the signal to start the cattle northward.

"The señora is well enough to travel?" he inquired solicitously. "She will be all right in the wagon?"

"I think so," Shannon said. "Of course, if she isn't she won't tell us, so we'll have to keep an eye on her. Now

154

let's get started—I want to reach Rancho Alvarez as soon as possible, and I know that the men are anxious to see their families again."

He looked around at the herd and at the waiting vaqueros.

"*Vamanos, amigos,*" he called. "We have a long way to ride."

And so they started for home, moving slowly as the sun rose higher and the dust puffed up under the feet of the plodding herd. Shannon had been a lawman all his life, and therefore had little firsthand experience of cattle drives, but there was something impressive about this living tide of men and animals moving deliberately and inexorably toward the far horizon. The days of the great Texas cattle drives were over, but as he rode easily beside the herd Shannon could feel something of what the men who first blazed the long, dusty trails from Texas to Kansas must have felt as they pushed their longhorn cattle north into history.

All that day and through the days following, they continued on their way. They traveled at a leisurely pace, for the cattle were thin and tired. The rustlers had driven the herd hard on their flight into Texas, and it had taken its toll on the animals. Because of this, Shannon wanted to make the trip as easy as possible for them.

Normally, trailing livestock would have been an unpleasant and even boring business, but in this case Shannon felt a sense of relief, as the very peacefulness of the passing hours began to ease the strain of the past days.

Under protest, Charlotte remained in the bed of the wagon, and Shannon made it a point to ride back periodically and look in on her. On one of these visits he found her sitting up, looking over the tailgate of the wagon at the New Mexico landscape sliding slowly away behind them.

"Where's Pepita?" Shannon said as he rode up and fell in behind the wagon. "She's supposed to be keeping an eye on you."

Charlotte laughed.

"She's riding in the chuck wagon," she said. "She's been fussing over me like the proverbial mother hen, and it's driving me crazy. I told her to go ride with the supplies and plan a particularly nice meal for the vaqueros tonight."

"Well," Shannon said, "just so you're all right."

"I've never felt better," she said cheerfully. "But I wish it weren't so far to Los Santos. Oh, Clay, it will be so good to be home."

"Not long now," said Shannon encouragingly. "We should be there in three or four days. Honestly, though, how are you feeling?"

"I'm fine," she said, lifting her arm. "See, no more sling. And I'm tired of sitting around like an invalid in this makeshift hearse. If you'll bring me my horse, I'll ride it through the gates of Rancho Alvarez like a normal human being."

"Patience, my dear," he said with a laugh. "Enjoy your leisure while you can."

"Some leisure," she said with a grimace. "I'm sick of bumping along back here. If you won't give me my horse,

I'm going to move up front and sit on the seat with the driver. I may even take the reins for awhile, just to have something to do."

Shannon shook his head in admiration. Charlotte was still full of the fire that had attracted him to her when they first met. He had never met anyone like her before, and he knew that he would never meet anyone like her again.

"Well," he said, "if you're going to drive, don't wander too far from the beaten path. The brush is pretty thick off the trail, and there are sinkholes out there big enough to swallow up the wagon—horses, driver, passenger, and all. The bushes make it hard to see them sometimes until it's too late."

"I'll be careful," she promised. She paused, looking at something back along the trail.

"Look," Charlotte said, pointing. "There's a rider coming up fast behind us."

"It's José Sanchez," Shannon said after a moment. "He's been riding drag at the rear of the herd." He slowed to wait for the vaquero.

Sanchez brought his horse to a sliding halt beside Shannon's buckskin.

*"Patrón!"* he cried. "Behind us! There is smoke!"

Shannon shaded his eyes and looked back along the trail. The vaquero was right—dirty wisps of black smoke were rising into the sky behind them.

"What is it, Clay?" Charlotte called. "What's wrong?"

Shannon did not reply. He had guessed the answer, and it made his stomach turn over.

"Ride up to the point and get Ramón," he said to Sanchez. "Bring him back here. Hurry."

He spurred the buckskin back along the trail, heading for the last rise over which they had traveled. When he reached it he reined his horse in and stared. A mile away, two at the most, a solid wall of smoke was billowing up above the brush. Beneath the smoke a line of orange flames could be seen coming rapidly at them along the ground they had just covered.

Ramón Peralta galloped up behind him.

"What is it, *Patrón?*" he asked.

"Brushfire," Shannon said in a taut voice. "And we're downwind of it. It's moving fast and it's coming in our direction."

Ramón caught his breath. *"Nombre de Dios!"* he muttered. A fire raging through the dry brush could panic the cattle, and if they could not get out of its path, it would destroy the entire herd.

"We must act quickly," he said. "What are your orders, *Patrón?*"

Shannon's thoughts raced furiously as he watched the fire. With the wind behind it, its progress toward them was far quicker than the herd was moving. Somehow they must put it out or at least delay it until the cattle could be gotten safely away. He knew that a few miles ahead of them the vegetation thinned out, and they would be moving into open country. If they could make it that far they would be safe, but at its present rate of progress the fire would overtake them long before they reached that point. Somehow, they had to buy some time.

"Get every man you can back here," he said. "Leave only enough with the herd to keep it moving. Tell the men you leave behind to push the cattle as hard as they can. Warn them to be alert, because if this fire gets close enough, the whole herd will stampede trying to get away from it."

"I will bring the men," Ramón said, swinging his horse's head about.

"One more thing," Shannon said. "Order the man driving the señora's wagon to whip up the horses and get her as far away as he can, as soon as he can. Tell him to move north, but to get off the trail so that if the herd does start to run, the wagon won't be caught in it. Quickly, *amigo*."

Ramón departed in a cloud of dust. Shannon waited on the rise, watching as the smoke and flames crawled nearer and nearer. The buckskin had picked up the scent of the fire now, and it began to move nervously under Shannon. He did his best to calm the stallion, all the while looking first back at the fire, then ahead to see if the vaqueros were coming to join him. Within a few minutes they appeared, riding at full gallop toward him.

"We are here, Señor," Ramón said as he rode up. "What is it that you wish us to do?"

"Our only chance of stopping that fire from reaching the herd is to make a firebreak," Shannon said. "We'll start cutting the brushwood and dragging the cuttings out of the path of the fire. We'll clear out an area as deep and as wide as we can manage. I don't know if we'll have enough time to make a breach large enough to stop the fire entirely, but perhaps we can at least slow it down."

Ramón repeated the instructions to the men.

"One more thing," Shannon said. "If we can't make a break wide enough to stop the fire by the time it's within a few hundred yards of us, we'll abandon the attempt. If that happens, ride like the wind back toward the herd. If you wait too long, the fire will overrun you and you will have no chance of survival. So please do as I say. I'd rather lose the herd than have anyone burned to death."

They went to work with desperate haste. Under Ramón's direction, some of the men set to work cutting bushes, while others used their lariats to drag the cuttings out of the way of the fire. The flames rushed ever closer to them as they worked, and soon greasy smoke was rolling over them, choking them with its acrid fumes.

They worked on feverishly trying to make the firebreak, but it quickly became evident to Shannon that the flames would overtake them before they would be able to clear enough of a space to stop the fire. Driven on by the heat of the fire, the wind was growing stronger. Its fitful gusts sent hot ashes swirling around the laboring men, and still-burning embers began to fall upon them. The horses were growing skittish with fright, and it soon became plain to Shannon that they were losing the race against time.

"It's no good," he said. "Let's get out of here."

They fled through the undergrowth, trying to outrun the fire. Within a few minutes they had caught up with the herd, and the vaqueros began to chivvy the cattle forward at a faster pace. Shannon's eyes narrowed as he saw that the wagon in which Charlotte was riding was still with the herd. He headed for it. No one was visible in the wagon bed, so he rode up to the front. Charlotte was on the seat beside the driver, peering anxiously back toward him.

"Antonio," Shannon shouted to the driver, "get this wagon moving. Put those horses into a dead run and get the señora out of here!"

"How bad is it, Clay?" Charlotte asked. Her face was drawn and anxious.

"Bad enough," Shannon replied. "The fire is catching up with us. We'll have to try to move the cattle faster. If I remember rightly, this underbrush thins out a little way ahead, and then we'll be in more open country. If we can make it that far, we'll have a chance."

"How can I help?" she said.

"You can help by getting out of danger," Shannon replied. "I want you away from here. The wagon can outrun the fire even if the cattle can't, and at least you'll be safe."

"But I want to stay with you," Charlotte said.

Shannon ignored her.

"Get going, Antonio," he ordered, "and don't stop until you're out of the brush country. Remember, the señora's life is in your hands."

"Never fear, Señor," Antonio said. "I will get her to safety!"

The wagon lurched forward and Shannon turned the buckskin back toward the rear of the herd to check the status of the fire.

The vaqueros were pushing the reluctant cattle as rapidly as they could. Shannon knew that, as tired as the animals were, some would soon begin to drop out into the thickets, where their chances of survival would be slim. He rode around the rear of the herd, urging cattle and vaqueros onward.

Then, just as he began to think that they might escape the fire after all, gunfire erupted at the front of the pack.

Shannon raced toward the sound. Ramón met him halfway.

"We have been ambushed, Señor!" he said. "Men were waiting for us up ahead, and they opened fire as we approached. Two of the vaqueros are down, but we are shooting back."

They put the horses at a dead run, hurrying toward the source of the gunfire. The cattle, becoming more and more fearful with the fire behind and the gunshots ahead, had ceased their forward progress and were milling around uneasily. Shannon could see that they were close to panicking.

"No one's watching the stock," Shannon said to Ramón as they galloped.

"The vaqueros have all gone forward to join the fight," Ramón shouted back.

A shiver ran down Shannon's spine. Whoever had ambushed them had robbed them of any chance of escape. The herd's forward progress had now stopped completely, and with no one to keep them together the cattle would soon scatter and be overwhelmed by the fire.

As Ramón had reported, the Alvarez men were all out

ahead, wheeling their horses about and firing their weapons rapidly. Two of the Alvarez vaqueros were on the ground; one of them was moving feebly, the other lay still.

About three hundred yards beyond the Alvarez men stood a grove of trees at the top of a little rise. Puffs of smoke in the trees revealed that the drygulchers, whoever they might be, were sheltering themselves in the grove and returning the vaqueros' fire with interest. As Shannon approached the vaqueros' position, bullets began to sing past him, as if the attackers were focusing their fire on him.

"They are shooting at you!" Ramón cried.

"They're shooting at all of us," Shannon replied, pulling his Winchester from its scabbard.

They joined the other vaqueros.

"Spread out!" Shannon shouted. "Don't give them an easy target. How many of them are there—can anybody see?"

"They've kept well under cover," someone said, "but there are at least ten. We've counted the flashes from their rifles."

"Any idea who they are?" Shannon asked, studying the distant treeline.

"No, *Patrón*," another vaquero said. "They are too far away for us to tell."

*Just as well that they are,* Shannon thought. *If they'd had the sense to wait until we were closer to them to open fire, they could have killed us all by now.*

"We can't move the cattle forward while they are shooting at us," Ramón said, "and the fire is behind us. We are trapped!"

Shannon closed his eyes briefly. Whatever he was going to do, he would have to do it soon. A few feet from him another vaquero cried out and fell from his horse under the hail of gunfire from the trees. It was apparent that a charge into the teeth of the bushwhackers' rifles would be suicidal. Yet when Shannon looked back he saw that the fire was now close to the rear of the rapidly panicking herd. They were on the edge of disaster; there was now only one choice.

"Ramón," he said, his voice hollow and his heart heavy, "we'll have to stampede the herd and drive them forward into the attackers."

"We will lose many animals if we do," Ramón warned.

"We'll lose them *all* if we don't," Shannon replied. "Follow me!"

He turned the buckskin once more and dashed headlong toward the rear of the herd with the Alvarez men close behind him. As they rode around behind the milling animals, the vaqueros looked over at Shannon, uncertain as to whether he really meant to stampede his own cattle. Shannon sheathed his Winchester and drew his six-gun, then took a deep breath. What he was about to do was a desperate measure indeed, one that might result in the loss of the entire herd. But there was no time for deliberation, for the crackle of flames could be heard clearly now as the fire drew nearer.

"Go!" Shannon shouted. He put the buckskin into a dead

run toward the rearmost of the cattle, whooping and firing into the air.

The stock, already on the verge of total panic, needed no further urging. Immediately they broke into a dead run, charging headlong away from the fire and from the gunshots and wild yells of the vaqueros behind them. Within moments the entire herd was fleeing full tilt up the trail. The thunder of their hooves drowned out both the gunshots and the roar of the approaching fire.

Shannon raced along beside them, urging them onward, reloading the Colt as he rode. He felt a sudden moment of concern as he remembered that Charlotte was somewhere nearby in the wagon. Had she gotten clear? He could only hope that she had, for nothing was going to stop the fear-maddened cattle now, and everything in their path would be pulverized beneath their flashing hooves.

They were fast approaching the trees from which the gunmen had ambushed them. In the grove, men were scattering like leaves, trying to escape the wall of bovine flesh that was bearing down on them. Shannon and the vaqueros swept into the midst of the gunmen, firing rapidly. One man was hiding behind a tree trunk just ahead of Shannon, shooting at them. Shannon swung the buckskin around the tree and shot the man through the heart. Someone else was firing at him from behind a rock, and Shannon sent two quick shots in his direction. The man howled in pain and vanished from sight.

Smoke and dust swirled heavily around them, adding to the unreality of the scene and making it difficult to distinguish friend from foe. The cattle were streaming past, crashing through the trees and undergrowth, unstoppable now in their flight. Shannon struggled to see through the murk, looking for more targets. Somewhere a horse squealed in terror, but Shannon could not tell whether the rider had been an Alvarez vaquero or one of the attackers.

The buckskin swerved aside to avoid trampling a dead body on the ground, and Shannon pulled the horse's head around to see who it was lying there. With a start he realized that the fallen man was one of the rustlers they had captured at Snyder's Texas hideout. He had been among those who escaped from the Casa Cochina jail with Snyder.

*So that's it,* Shannon thought. *The fire was no accident. They planned this, all of it—fire, ambush, and all. They intended to kill every one of us and take the herd again.*

The old anger welled up within him.

*You've crossed my trail once too often, Snyder,* he thought to himself. *This time there'll be no quarter, no mercy, and no trial by jury.*

Over the hubbub of the shooting and the fleeing cattle, Shannon heard a woman's voice calling his name. He turned and saw a wagon bouncing toward him over the rough ground. Charlotte was in the driver's seat, holding the reins and urging the sweating horses onward. She pulled up beside him, fighting to control the agitated team.

"Who is it?" she asked, indicating the dead man on the ground.

"One of Snyder's men," Shannon said, again reloading the Colt.

"Snyder?" said Charlotte, aghast. "He's here?"

"I haven't seen him yet," Shannon said, "but he's here, all right. They deliberately set the fire to draw us back to the rear of the herd, then opened up on us from the trees ahead. It was a perfect setup. They must have known we were shorthanded and decided to have another crack at stealing the herd."

The cattle were still streaming past and the dust and smoke billowed around Shannon and Charlotte, half-blinding them. A man came running toward them out of the trees, his revolver raised to shoot. Charlotte saw him before Shannon did. Dropping the reins, she seized a rifle from the wagon boot and fired. The man dropped as if poleaxed and lay still.

"Nice shot," Shannon said, a little shaken at the nearness of the encounter.

"I told you I could be useful on this trip," Charlotte replied with a tight smile.

"Where's Antonio?" Shannon asked suddenly, realizing for the first time that Charlotte was alone.

"We hit a pothole while we were trying to get out of the way of the stampeding herd," Charlotte answered, putting down the rifle. "Antonio fell off, and by the time I could get the horses under control I had lost sight of him. I think the cattle trampled him."

"They may trample us too if we don't get out of here," Shannon said, kicking the buckskin to one side as a handful of wild-eyed steers rushed past and vanished into the smoke. Shannon moved the stallion into the shelter of the wagon as another group of cattle pounded past them, and then another. After that no further animals appeared.

"I think that's the last of them," Shannon said, "but there's still the fire to worry about. Look, you'd better take the wagon and get out of these trees before the flames reach them. I'll go back and look for Antonio."

"The fire is too close, Clay. You'll be trapped by it."

"I have to go, Charlotte. I can't leave one of our men back there to die."

"But. . . ."

"Go on, Charlotte, please. I'll be all right. Get out of these woods, into the open area ahead. Then wait for me. Go on, there's no need to worry. I don't plan to be barbecued this week."

## Chapter Nineteen

As soon as Charlotte had turned the wagon and started toward safety, Shannon galloped out of the trees and back down the slope. The air was hot and thick with smoke and ashes, and he could hear the crackle of the flames as they marched forward through the dry thickets. Shannon weaved the buckskin back and forth through the brush, calling Antonio's name, but there was no reply.

A horseman materialized out of the smoke. At first Shannon thought that the missing vaquero, Antonio, might have found a riderless horse and commandeered it, but he quickly realized that the rider was the Alvarez foreman, Ramón Peralta.

"I am glad that you are unharmed, *Patrón*," Ramón said, knocking some hot ash from his clothing. "The señora—is she all right?"

"Yes," Shannon said. "I just left her in that grove of trees with the wagon. The man who was driving the wagon, Antonio, was thrown off the seat while they were trying to avoid the fire. I'm looking for him now."

"I will help you," Ramón replied. "But we have very little time before the flames reach us."

They searched for several more minutes, but the smoke was now very thick. Both men were coughing, and their frightened horses were becoming almost unmanageable.

"It is no use, Señor," Ramón said. "You cannot find Antonio in all this. Let us take ourselves to safety. Later, perhaps, when the fire has burned itself out, we can come back to look for him."

Reluctantly, Shannon started up the hill toward the grove of trees, Ramón beside him. The smoke followed them.

"The Señora," Ramón said. "You say she is driving the wagon herself?"

"Yes. She's taking it on into the open country, where she'll be clear of the fire. Don't worry, Ramón, she's fine. Our main worry now is recovering the cattle."

"I've sent the vaqueros to try to catch up to them," Ramón said. "Who was it that ambushed us?"

"It was Snyder and his gang," Shannon replied, slapping at an ember that was burning a hole in his shirt. "They followed us and set the fire to box us in, then moved ahead and hid in the trees, knowing we'd ride right into their guns trying to save the herd. A clever plan. Fortunately, they bungled it."

"They have paid for their stupidity," Ramón said with satisfaction.

"Did any of them get away?"

"I think not," Ramón said. "We caught one or two of them, but they will not trouble us again." He touched his knife meaningfully.

They reached the top of the rise and entered the grove. A few yards into the trees Ramón abruptly reined up, staring at something ahead of them.

"What is it?" Shannon asked, trying to see through the stinging smoke.

"L-look, Señor!" Ramón stammered, pointing.

Shannon looked in the direction indicated. Snyder was standing under one of the trees with his six-gun in his hand and a leer on his face. Shannon's first reaction was to reach for his Colt, but as he started to do so his hand froze above the holster and cold fear gripped his heart. Snyder was standing next to a very nervous horse, holding the reins tightly to keep the animal from bolting. On the horse's back sat Charlotte, with her hands tied behind her and a noose pulled tight around her neck. The rope had been thrown over a large branch above Charlotte's head, then tied around the trunk of the tree just under the branch. Charlotte's hat was missing, and a trickle of blood was running down one cheek.

"Clay!" she shouted. "Go back! It's Snyder!"

"Shut up, you. . . ," Snyder said. "Well, Shannon, we meet again. Only this time it ain't in no livery stable, and you're going to be the one who does the suffering."

Shannon stared at the rivulet of red on Charlotte's face.

"Snyder," he said, his voice shaking with emotion, "if you've harmed her, you're going to find out what suffering really is."

"Oh, I haven't hurt her yet," Snyder said. "Not much, anyway. But I will, Shannon. I will, unless you and your Mex friend there drop your guns on the ground right now."

"Don't do it, Clay!" Charlotte cried. "He'll kill you."

Shannon's head was spinning. All he could see was Charlotte's face and the rope around her neck. It was as if he had suddenly been transported into the middle of his own worst nightmare.

"Let her go, Snyder," he said in a choked voice. "This is between you and me."

Snyder's mouth twitched into a malevolent smile.

"You're right there." He smirked. "Dead right. I'm going to kill you, Shannon. I said I would, back in Casa Cochina. You killed my men and took the cattle I was gonna sell, then you made me ride upside down on my belly for a hundred miles and stuck me in that stinking jail. You owe me plenty, law dog, and now I'm going to collect it. In spades."

"Collect it from me, then, not my wife. Let her go."

"Not a chance," Snyder said. "Not until I settle my score with you. Now shuck those guns, or else."

Charlotte twisted her head, struggling to speak clearly despite the pressure of the rough rope against her throat.

"Don't do it, Clay," she said. "He'll gun you down the minute you do."

"Think about it, Shannon," Snyder said jubilantly. "If you try to draw that fancy six-gun you're wearing, I'll slap this horse on the rump and your lady friend here will be dancing on thin air. She won't look so pretty with that rope choking the life out of her."

"Shoot him, Clay!" Charlotte said defiantly. "He's going to kill me anyway."

"Make up your mind, Shannon," Snyder rasped. "You or her—take your choice."

Shannon wavered, trying to decide what to do. He realized that Charlotte was probably right—once he and Ramón dropped their guns, there would be nothing to stop Snyder from killing all of them. But Shannon also knew with absolute certainty that if he and Ramón did not comply with Snyder's demand, the outlaw would carry out his threat to hang Charlotte. The thought of Charlotte's body jerking at the end of the rope was more than Shannon could bear. He would take any risk, die himself if necessary, to avoid that.

"Drop your gunbelt, Ramón," Shannon said, despair in his voice. "He'll kill her if we don't."

Slowly, they undid their gunbelts and let them fall to the ground.

"Now climb off those horses and move away from them," Snyder said. Seething with rage, Shannon dismounted. Ramón followed, his dark eyes fixed with burning hatred on Snyder all the while.

"All right, Snyder," Shannon said. "Our guns are on the ground and so are we. Turn the woman loose."

Snyder's laugh was high and cracked, the laugh of a madman.

"Did you really believe I'd do that?" he said, chortling. "You're an even bigger fool than I thought, Shannon. I ain't gonna let her go. I've got you now—you and her both. And I'm gonna kill you both, real slow."

He looked up at Charlotte with an unholy light in his eyes.

"When I caught her I would have killed her straight out," he said, "but I wanted to keep her alive just for this. She put up quite a fight when I grabbed her. Nearly scratched my eyes out. I had to pistol-whip her a couple of times to calm her down and get her up on the horse. But now I've got you both right where I want you, Mr. U.S. Marshal, you and your Spanish wildcat. So, Shannon, you ready to watch her die?"

"Let her go," Shannon pleaded. He had never begged anyone for anything before in his life, but he was ready to go to any lengths to save Charlotte. "Come on, Snyder," he said. "She's got nothing to do with this. It's me you want."

"Yeah." Snyder laughed. "It's you I want, and I'm going to have you, too—right after this witch dies."

"At least give us a chance," Shannon said. "We'll make it just the two of us, Snyder, you and me, face to face—guns, fists, anything you like."

"Oh, no." Snyder chuckled, his eyes gleaming with malevolence. "I'd be a fool to give you a chance. But I'm a fair man, so I'll give you a choice. Your choice is, I can start the horse slow, so it drags her off and she strangles, or I can start the horse fast, so she breaks her neck. Which will it be, Shannon? Fast or slow?"

"He means it," Shannon said to Ramón. "He's going to hang her and shoot us."

"What can we do?" said Ramón. "Our guns are out of reach."

Shannon's fevered brain was forming a plan. It was a desperate gamble, one with little possibility of success, but there was no alternative. Any chance was better than none at all.

"Ramón," Shannon whispered, "exactly how good are you with that knife?"

"You have seen me use it, *Patrón,*" Ramón replied, puzzled. "I have killed more than one man with it in your service."

"Yes," Shannon said, "but that was always up close. Can you hit something with it from a distance?"

"Certainly, Señor. I can put it through his heart easily from here."

"No, that's no good," Shannon said. "Even with a knife in his chest, a man can take a long time to die—long enough to slap a horse on the rump, at least."

"Then what . . . ?"

"The rope, Ramón. Can you throw the knife and cut the rope from where we're standing?"

Ramón swallowed hard.

"Very difficult, Señor. And if I miss, he will surely start the horse and kill her."

"She's as good as dead anyway," Shannon said, "and you and I will be next. None of us has a lot to lose at this point."

"Then I will try, Señor," he said, crossing himself. "Tell me when."

"Soon," Shannon said. "Be ready."

"What're you two talking about?" Snyder snarled. "You ain't got nothin' to talk about. The time for talkin's over. Ready, Shannon? Ready to hear her gurgle?"

Shannon's muscles tensed. His eyes met Charlotte's, and he gave her a barely perceptible nod of his head. Charlotte understood. Without hesitation she twisted her body in the saddle, pulling her foot free of the stirrup. Though Snyder had tied her hands, he had made the mistake of leaving her legs free, and with all her strength she kicked out at him, driving her spur into his face. Snyder screamed and staggered back. Then, roaring blasphemies, he lunged forward again and smashed the barrel of his six-gun hard against the horse's flank.

At Charlotte's first movement, Shannon flung himself upon the ground, reaching out for his discarded gunbelt. His hand closed around the handle of the Colt and he ripped it from its holster, his thumb drawing back the hammer as the gun barrel cleared the leather.

Before Shannon's body even hit the earth, Ramón whipped his knife out of its sheath and hurled it. The blade sped through the air and buried itself in the tree trunk. As the point of the knife sank itself into the wood, the edge sliced through the rope precisely where it was tied around the tree, cutting the fibers completely. The severed rope came free of the trunk just as the horse bolted. But although the cord was no longer secured to the tree, it was still looped over the branch above Charlotte's head, and for a terrible moment Shannon was afraid that the rope dragging across the branch would catch on the bark and pull Charlotte backward over the horse's withers. Then the rope was free, and Charlotte was leaning forward in the saddle, somehow managing to keep her seat on the plunging animal despite her tied hands.

Snyder was still standing beside the tree, pressing his hand against his cheek where Charlotte had slashed him with her spur. His eyes were wide and his mouth was open as he stood momentarily frozen in disbelief at this sudden reversal of fortune. Then he uttered a screech of pure hatred and raised his six-gun to fire at Charlotte's back.

Methodically, Shannon pumped six shots into Snyder's body, driving him back against the tree trunk. The outlaw's revolver went flying as he hung there for a moment, spread-eagled against the tree, then crumpled slowly to the ground like a rag doll suddenly deprived of its stuffing.

So intense was Shannon's fury that he continued to cock the Colt and pull the trigger even after the weapon was empty and Snyder lay motionless upon the ground. Again and again Shannon thumbed the hammer without effect as he advanced, half-blinded by smoke and his own rage, toward Snyder's sprawled body.

Ramón grasped Shannon's arm and gently took the smoking six-gun from his hand.

"Enough, *Patrón*," he said. "The man is dead."

Slowly, the red mist began to clear from Shannon's brain.

"Charlotte," he said thickly, still in a daze. "Is she . . . ?"

"She is here," said Ramón, gesturing. Despite her tethered hands, Charlotte had managed to guide the horse back to them and was just sliding down from the saddle. She was breathing rapidly, but seemed to be otherwise unharmed. Ramón removed the noose from around her neck, then retrieved his knife from the tree and cut the cord that was binding her wrists. As soon as her hands were free, Charlotte ran to Shannon and wrapped her arms around him. Tears of relief coursed down her cheeks as the two of them clung together.

They remained thus for a moment, everything else forgotten, holding each other close as the tension of the past minutes slowly faded. Then they stepped apart again, each feeling the exhilaration of those who have stood without hope on the brink of eternity and have somehow miraculously survived.

During their embrace, Ramón had moved tactfully away to inspect Snyder's body and gather up the riderless horses. Then he returned, smiling broadly.

"Thanks be to God that you are unharmed, Señora," he said, handing Shannon the buckskin's reins.

"Thank you, Ramón," Charlotte said huskily. "We are all very fortunate." Then she noticed that the old vaquero's hands were trembling. She herself was badly shaken by what had happened, but she quickly demonstrated that she had not lost her sense of humor.

Wiping away her tears, she smiled at Ramón.

"I'm glad you weren't trembling like that when you threw the knife at that rope, Ramón," she said jokingly.

Ramón looked at her with a crooked smile.

"Ah, but I was, Señora," he said. "Believe me, I was."

# Chapter Twenty

Shannon and Charlotte stood a moment longer by the wagon, slowly recovering from their close encounter with death. Gradually, they became aware that the smoke from the fire was still drifting around them.

"Forgive me," Ramón said, looking back down the slope, "but we must go now. The fire still burns behind us. It is dying down at last, but we would be wise to move out of its way nonetheless."

Quickly Shannon mounted the buckskin while Charlotte took Ramón's horse. Ramón climbed onto the seat of the wagon and whipped up the team.

"The cattle," Charlotte said as they started to follow the wagon down the far slope of the ridge. "Are they safe?"

"Most of them, I think," Shannon said. "The open country is just ahead, and the herd was moving in that direction.

180

The fire will burn itself out before it reaches them."

"We're going to have a time of it rounding them up," said Charlotte. "They'll be scattered over many miles."

Shannon's jaw tightened.

"We'll find them," he said calmly. "We'll find them, and then we'll go home."

They set up an impromptu camp beyond reach of the dying brushfire and began to count their losses—and their blessings. As far as Shannon could determine from talking with the vaqueros, all of the outlaws who had ambushed them had died in the gun battle or been trampled to death by the stampeding herd. The Alvarez losses were two killed and three wounded. They thought that Antonio, the man who fell off Charlotte's wagon, might be dead also, but he came walking into camp an hour before sunset, singed and footsore but very much alive. The chuck wagon appeared shortly thereafter, with Pepita Lopez sitting beside the driver. Pepita was quite disappointed when Shannon explained to her that the rustlers, including Snyder, were all dead, and that there was no one left to hang. However, after Shannon described Snyder's death to her, she soon regained her good spirits and went cheerfully to work feeding the men.

It took them two days to round up the scattered herd. When they finally concluded that there was no point in searching any further, they gathered back at the camp and prepared to set out again for Rancho Alvarez. By the best count they could make, a little over a hundred head had been lost in the stampede. Altogether, of the two-thousand-plus cattle that Snyder and his men had stolen and taken to Texas, less than nine hundred would return to their home range.

"It could have been worse, I suppose," Shannon said. "All told, we lost over a thousand head, but we still have several thousand on the north range and more west of the Rio Verde, so we won't exactly starve next winter."

"And we're alive," Charlotte said, her eyes shining. "That's the most important thing. We're alive, and we're together."

Thus they resumed their journey homeward.

## Chapter Twenty-one

Once again, Shannon and Charlotte stood on the second-floor balcony of the great house at Rancho Alvarez. Their Texas adventure had begun many days before with the viewing of a sunrise, but this time it was evening, and they were on the west side of the house watching the sunset.

Beyond the walls of the garden that surrounded the house, cattle were grazing peacefully, and nearby in the bunkhouse someone was strumming a guitar while several vaqueros sang softly to celebrate their homecoming. It was an idyllic scene, in sharp contrast to the strain and violence of the past few days. Shannon put his arm around Charlotte and held her close to his side as the two of them listened to the music and watched the sun sinking slowly toward the horizon in an another awe-inspiring display of color.

"What was the telegram that came from town a little while ago?" Charlotte asked.

Shannon laughed.

"Ears," he said.

*"What?"* Charlotte said, startled.

"Sorry," Shannon said. "It's a sort of joke. The lieutenant who helped us at Fort Lister said that if the army's inspector general chopped off that crooked colonel's head, the lieutenant would send us his ears."

"And did he?" Charlotte asked, puzzled. She was still not quite sure if Shannon was joking.

"No," Shannon said, "he didn't send me anyone's ears, but he sent me the telegram to let me know that the officer in question has been shipped back to Washington for court-martial. That's good news, because otherwise, as a United States marshal, I would have had to go back there to deal with the situation. Fortunately, the army has taken care of its own problem."

"Then it's really over?" said Charlotte, gazing anxiously up at him.

"Yes," Shannon said, smiling down at her. "It's over— finally."

"I'm so glad," she murmured, nestling her head on his shoulder. "It all seems like a bad dream now, doesn't it?"

"It was real enough at the time," Shannon replied. "But we're home now, and the nightmare is over."

"Home," Charlotte said. "What a beautiful word. I love it so here, Clay. At times in the past few weeks I thought we might never see it again."

"Well, we're here now," said Shannon. "And the badge is back in the drawer as I promised."

"I don't suppose it will stay there forever," she said, looking up at him affectionately, "but I'm content just to be here with you now, even if it's only for a little while."

She sighed wistfully.

"We've fought so hard, haven't we, Clay?" she said. "We've fought so many times for Rancho Alvarez and for the right to live out our lives here in peace. I pray that we never have to fight anyone again."

"You always have to fight to keep what's yours," Shannon said. "No matter how much or how little you have, there's always somebody who wants to take it away from you. Unfortunately, that's the way of the world."

"Then we'll keep fighting," said Charlotte firmly. "For as long as it takes."

"Yes," Shannon said, "we'll keep fighting. This place, this way of life, is worth fighting for."

For a few minutes more they stood there, silently watching as the sun disappeared behind the hills. Then, as twilight stole over Rancho Alvarez, Shannon leaned down and kissed his wife softly on the lips, and they walked back across the balcony into the house, hand in hand, just as Charlotte had said—alive and together.

2011

2010

2009

2007

2004

2006

2003